A SURE THING

A SURE THING

Racketeers, Romance, and Racehorses
Rush To The Finish Line

VINCENT J. CINCOTTA

ARPress
45 Dan Road Suite 5
Canton MA 02021

Hotline: 1(888) 821-0229
Fax: 1(508) 545-7580

Ordering Information:
Quantity sales.Special discounts are available on quantity purchases by corporations, associations, and others.For details, contact the publisher at the address above.

Printed in the United States of America.

ISBN-13:   Paperback   979-8-89389-200-0
                eBook   979-8-89389-201-7
                Hardback   979-8-89389-202-4

Library of Congress Control Number: 2024905199

Tabel Of Contents

The Foreword vii

Chapter 1   Uncle Vito 1

Chapter 2   The Early Years 11

Chapter 3   The Military 19

Chapter 4   Another World—High Society 25

Chapter 5   Home Coming 33

Chapter 6   A Groom 41

Chapter 7   The Trainer 46

Chapter 8   The Scratch 55

Chapter 9   Romance Is in the Air 64

Chapter 10   Jockeys 69

Chapter 11   Suzanne and Raymond Connect 72

Chapter 12   Back to the Party 83

Chapter 13   An Evil Visitor 87

Chapter 14   Suzanne Comforts 92

Chapter 15   Father and Daughter 100

Chapter 16   Developing a Racehorse 104

Chapter 17   Ladies Chatting 108

Chapter 18   A New Jockey 112

Chapter 19   A Sure Thing Races Again 118

Chapter 20   A Long Night 126

Chapter 21   The Police Arrived 132

Chapter 22   Suzanne Finds Out 135

Chapter 23   Charles Objects 140

Chapter 24   Another Afternoon of Racing 145

Chapter 25   The Triple Crown Campaign 148

Chapter 26   The Derby 151

Chapter 27   The Morning After 155

Chapter 28   The Preakness 160

Chapter 29   The Belmont.. 164

The Foreword

*T*his thriller romance, with a racetrack backdrop, depicts a journey on the trail of uncertainty for the main character as he seeks to find his destiny in life. Although under different circumstances, have we not all been on that road?

He must survive the powerful struggle of a young love that is seriously challenged by the standards of an impenetrable High Society.

The development of a champion racehorse, beclouded with the violent, brazen intrusion of the underworld into the racing world and the lover's lives, evolves as the intrigue develops.

These aspects are all authentically intertwined with the realistic everyday events of Thoroughbred racing, the Sport of Kings, the oldest sport in America.

Please, when you finish reading the book, come join me in the Winner's Circle for a photograph.

CHAPTER 1
Uncle Vito

The six flickering amber lights outside and above the sign of Di Mario Ristorante, located on Fourth Avenue near Shore Road in Brooklyn, strained to be clearly seen. Precipitation fog mixed with moderate rain filled the chilly night air. For the prudent patron, this was a raincoat, umbrella evening. On any busy weekend, this twenty-two-table restaurant with a well-stocked bar of Italian wines and liqueurs could easily hold well over a hundred customers simultaneously. None of them ever minded waiting at the bar for a table to become available. It was a social event.

Sal, the bartender, sang lines from Italian songs as he poured drinks while most of the mingling crowd were locals who knew each other. Strangers became friends quickly with anyone around them, which made the lounge area a perfect setting for an impromptu party. Since this was a weekday hampered by the inclement weather, the establishment was handling slightly under half capacity or less. The bar space empty except for one lonely widower wondering why? However, the other people who ventured out for a relaxing evening, disregarding the weather, took full advantage of the savory selections; the mellow vino; and the intimate, heart-tingling conversations. If children were at the table, as some were, the down-to-earth talks were less spicy. Who was cheating on whom was never discussed.

Inside the restaurant, Vito Di Mario, the owner, and godfather of the La Matta Mafia family, had chosen to sit comfortably at a six-capacity table in the rear of the dining room with a wall behind it. Although only occasionally at this restaurant, when he was there, his presence could be strongly felt. If sitting alone, his eyes scanned the working staff and dinners, looking for anything noteworthy. A nod to the maître d' brought him on the run to Vito's table, and whatever needed to be corrected was rectified immediately. Occasionally, a bottle of wine to certain table was the task to be carried out.

When entertaining anyone at the restaurant, the godfather controlled the conversation with stories, questions, and sound advice. Those with him listened with interest; it was wise to do so, especially if they wanted a return invitation. Paying attention had rewards.

Dinning and entertaining at the same location afforded Vito a logistically protected position with a full view of the premises, customers, and activity. Other tables of various sizes in the immediate vicinity were deliberately left vacant on that slow night. The godfather wanted privacy, preferring to speak informally to his special guest inside the spacious family restaurant rather than in the confines of his crowded second floor office. This important meeting with Tommy Z, the head of the Genova family, had been set up the day before. Occasionally, Vito visually checked the expensive 1959 Italian-designed Gio Ponti wall clock to keep track of the appointed arrival time.

The serious purpose of this talk was to make certain that this underworld paisano, clearly understood what position he held regarding an explosive personal issue that involved his only nephew, Raymond, with some members of the Genova gang.

Although Vito was tough, his immediate family always received attention. Whenever help was needed, he made sure that it happened, but often those protected never knew of his involvement. This was the way it had to be, quick and quiet! His brother-in-law, Sean, Josephine's husband, operated a small printing business, which realized some rough times. Yet, when through the years as these crises arose, a large order surprisingly came out of nowhere into the office. Sean never could figure out where the new accounts originated. Behind the scenes, Vito had leaned on someone.

When presenting his request to them for an order, yes was the only acceptable answer. Who wanted to be on the other side of Vito's facial expression when it spoke of displeasure. A first cousin, Louie, operated a twelve-man auto mechanic shop in Sheepshead Bay, Brooklyn, where some workers wanted to unionize the place. This basically would have priced the relative out of business! For reasons unknown, the union's interest to organize those people came to a fast halt. The labor organizers suddenly left the auto shop's perimeter, saving the relative. When a benevolent Vito sent family members or especially close friends who needed loans to a certain bank in Bensonhurst, Brooklyn, these people were made to feel warmly welcomed, a reassuring feeling to start with when searching for cash. They were never denied.

The stories of Vito's unknown deeds go on and on! Again, he never sought or demanded acknowledgment, but should gratitude be shown, a gift box of quality—Maduro Robusto cigars—said it all. Vito's white long-sleeved shirt pocket always carried three. Although, childhood friends since age seven, Vito and Tommy had joined different crime families, each climbing to the top, yet they stayed close.

This life-long connection became unbreakable when they were young. It happened on an early August morning, after hitching a ride to Jacob Reiss Park, Queens, New York, when Vito, at fifteen, saved Tommy from drowning. Swimming in about twelve feet of water while on the far side of the breaking waves, Tommy had an excruciating leg cramp and was helpless. The lifeguards were not yet on duty therefore, Vito struggled alone to bring his friend back to shallow water! Exhausted, they barely made it! Thereafter, for that and a multiple of other reasons, they stayed bonded, closer than brothers, respecting each other. On occasions, through the years, they had profitable business dealings together. The initial greeting flattered the arriving guest. "Tommy, you look great!" The host continued, "What's your secret?" Equally at ease, Tommy joked, "It must be . . . clean living."

Vito gave him a sly, you-got-to-be-kidding-me smile then graciously thanked him for coming. Dismissing a need to be grateful, Tommy countered with a "Hell, it's always good to spend time with an old friend. There aren't many around. Anyway . . . anyway, I expect your call."

Proudly, dinner was offered as Vito squarely placed a colorful, large two-fold menu in his friend's hand. The host waited and watched for a moment, but Tommy declined to open it. The guest wasn't hungry, offering the excuse that he had eaten an earlier dinner at home with his wife, Teresa. Besides, it would be better to immediately talk about the business at hand if Vito did not have an objection. Leaning over to be nearer with the man on his left, Vito spoke in a low, deliberate tone, "Yeah, to talk right now is no problem. Better this way. Why should there be tension between friends?"

Moving even inches closer to Tommy's right ear, he added, "Listen. I'm not going to judge what happened to my nephew, Raymond. In our way of life, we do what we gotta do, but when that young guy is involved, so am I! More directly, let's say I am him, and nobody is ever taking advantage of me! That's the way I live . . . and you know me." Tommy agreed. "If not, by now, after forty-five years, it will never happen, and we don't ever want any bad blood between us . . . Go on." The talker drew a deep breath. He wasn't close to being finished. "You run your organization and me . . . mine. We have a lot of things to consider, try and keep everybody in line, bring cash to the table, make things move ahead. It ain't easy, but my concern here is that I want Raymond safe! What physically happened yesterday at the racetrack between your boys and Raymond can never happen again!"

The barrage continued, "Bruno and his ape cousin are two mooks who never should have gone to Raymond's with their dirty work in the first place. Didn't they know who he was? How come? Does this kid need to carry a sign on his back that says, Vito's nephew'? If I had found out what was going on early enough, it would have been stopped. This combination was no good for nobody right from the start. The racetrack must have two hundred trainers, why pick on him? Raymond isn't paying with his life for their stupid mistakes, the assholes!" "Friend, I hear you. Now listen to me. This racing game is a complicated deal . . . I've let Bruno and his crew run it. From what I understand, they got some top jocks, a couple of trainers, a veterinarian, and drug suppliers in their pockets. Who knows how they juggle these pieces to put them straight. They are there every day, so it seemed smart to leave them alone. Besides, Bruno has made big money with it for us, and now, I have this ugly problem involving your nephew."

Vito shifted his body. "I got a good idea what happened. My nephew was clean. They wanted to hide behind his reputation and throw him a bone . . . What big-hearted idiots! Why him? Hustle somebody else! He doesn't want to be any part of them or our world! You can bet on it! How many times, do I have to say that the dumb fuckers made a big mistake, and they may end up paying for it?" The speech giver then relaxed in his chair, sat back, crossed his legs, waiting for a favorable response. Rubbing his white napkin with short strokes against the golden tablecloth, Tommy smoothly objected, "Now, Vito, you said you wouldn't judge . . . but you are. Can you see that?"

Willing to accept his friend's criticism without question, Vito straightened up and continued, "Okay, I won't take a side anymore, only plain and simple talk. I need you to tell Bruno, his goon Sonny, and anybody else who needs to hear it . . . that if anything happens to Raymond . . . they will regret it! This is, regardless of what they think, needs to get done to make things straight! They can do what they want, but they can't touch the kid. Hands off! There's no give on that. I'm like a rock! As far as what already went down . . . well, it can be forgotten . . . done. Mistakes happen!"

"Yeah, I made a few in my life," admitted Tommy. The guest then looked Vito directly in the eyes. "I can understand your strong message, backing you up some, but no guarantee on the outcome. There are hotheads out there who do crazy things. I can't watch everybody all the time. You know how that game goes . . . Somebody gets drunk, impulsive, he's out of control, and things get wild. This off-the-wall wacko is gonna be in big trouble with me, but the damage can't get undone. This is no easy position for me to be in!"

Conversely, Tommy let the severity of the situation come to the surface. "My boys have put guys away for less than this with my blessing. Now they want action. They are screaming for blood! A ton of money was lost, even our network in Las Vegas was ready to pounce on it. Vito, you know chances like this don't happen every day. Everybody is upset.

A lot of work and money went into the fix. My final decision must be handled carefully! I can't look weak! What am I talking about that you don't know as good as me?" There was no backing down from this tough uncle. "I understand, but . . . bad break for your guys. Sometimes things don't play out the way we figure." Vito's strong hands pressed hard on the table's edge, causing it to move. Tommy looked down, but his body's position remained unchanged. The speaker rolled on, "Regardless of what happens if this boy should happen to be hurt . . . be sure that Bruno and Sonny are gonna be hurt more! If my nephew is killed, those two with their balls cut off will be found dead together in the trunk of a stolen car down at Coney Island! This would not be a good ending for nobody . . . right? Who wants this! I see no other way out!"

Tommy listened with total attentiveness to Vito's position, which had been explicitly clear. The quest moved his head up and down several times during the detailed ultimatum, expressing some agreement on the spot on the strong points made but failed to answer Vito's last question.

For the proficient talker, that wasn't necessary. The host sensed he had achieved his objective. "My pitch is finished. You know what I'm talking about. If this was one of your nephews in trouble with my boys, you would be saying the same thing to me, and I would hear it out! Cumpa, your help is needed. Do me this favor. Don't let my nephew be a target!"

The visitor gave a short up-and-down head bow while extending the open palms of his stretched hands in Vito's direction. Safety from harm was assured, but that was where it stopped. "That's good enough for me. Now, come on. Have something to eat. The food here is spectacular. I should know. I own the damn place." It took Tommy less than a second to give in. "I'm not on a diet this week. How about a cannoli and espresso?" The restaurateur was openly pleased. He got his way. "Good choice. You must have read my mind. I'll have the same."

The owner silently motioned to a cute, young, shapely redhaired waitress who was anxiously waiting nearby to be called. To serve these powerful men made her day, and for certain, Tommy would leave a big tip. The top bosses always did; it was somewhere in their code of honor or hidden in their DNA. While eating dessert, the Mafia men laughed, recalling their wild youth, past ventures, and associates, some no longer around. The earlier serious conversation was completely dropped. It seemed to be in the distant past or as if it had never occurred, not an easy trick to pull off. They separated with the same friendship as when they first sat down. They hugged, kissed on the cheeks, and parted, slapping each other on the back.

Tommy's last gesture at the table was to take a hundred-dollar bill from his wallet and place it next to the empty espresso cup. "For the girl. She is nice." Slowly, Tommy, while casually walking out of the establishment, adjusted his tie then picked up his coat at the hat check, leaving a twenty-spot in the tip dish. He showed the same demeanor that would be displayed by any satisfied customer. There wasn't the slightest hint regarding the serious nature of his visit, that lives hung in the balance and hundreds of thousands of dollars, were blown as fast as the snap of a finger.

Directly outside of the restaurant sat a rain-drenched 1965 black Lincoln Continental, with suicide rear doors, parked illegally by a fire hydrant. The two men, sitting in the front seat behind a haze-covered windshield, smoked cigarettes; but as Tommy reached the vehicle, one of them got out, stepped on his smoke against the wet pavement, and opened the back door for his boss. No words were exchanged.

Alone, while still at his favorite spot in the restaurant, the recently energized Vito became unusually pensive, starting to recall his earlier life in Flatbush, living with his parents; sister, and his brother-in-law; and eventually Raymond. The key figure of the previous conversation soon came to mind. Fond thoughts of his nephew as a cute and inquisitive youngster was the way he visualized him that night.

Life for Vito had moved quickly, but the remembrances of his own vivid past remained. The longer he remained at the empty table, the deeper and clearer were the flashbacks of his youth, working as a longshoreman on the Brooklyn docks, getting involved in the mob while still sharing life with his immediate family at home. For Vito, these were truly the good old times that could not come back, but the strong memory of them would never fade away.

He recalled what was perhaps the best block in Brooklyn—East Twenty-Ninth Street, between Avenue P. and Quentin Road—lined on both sides by tall trees, which formed a canopy over the street. Most of the single-family homes had spacious, sloping front lawns while, at the end of the block, on the right-hand side near Avenue P. were four solidly built two-family red-brick homes with smaller level lawn areas. The Di Mario's house, which was one of them, had eight rooms on each floor, with a finished basement.

His parents were living in that house when Vito himself was born. Let us say that, as the years went by, the Di Mario family got their money's worth by using their home to maximum capacity. At times, there were as many as four closely related families living on the three levels with a combined number of thirteen people. They fashioned their lifestyle of several families living together as was customary in Italy, which gave these owners deep pride in themselves; being able to mirror the Old Country Ways in their New Homeland. It gave them a feeling of still having a connection to their roots.

On any given night, one of the ladies might prepare a fantastic homecooked Italian meal whose delightful aroma filled the air. Everyone in the house enjoyed those special selections, which were shared in the spirit of family togetherness. More joviality was impossible to find in any home or better food anywhere in the world! The special meal's main ingredient was always the same, an extra pinch of TLC.

Family to them was everything. No group was more congenial or respectful to each other, and even Vito found these loving traits to be somewhat of a sobering anchor of sanity as he dove into the underworld. Vito always knew that this special house was full of warmth. Everyone got along, regarded the other's space while there was never a clash of personalities. Added to that, each floor had only one bathroom, yet these amazing people happily shared all of life's aspects together.

Somehow, they made it work. Showers were always quick. The above became possible when the head of this family, Anthony Di Mario, and his lovely petite wife, Rose Oresci, were married in Sicily at the young ages of twenty-one and seventeen respectively. Soon after immigrating to New York City, they rented a one-bedroom flat in a crowded, noise-filled five-story-high tenement building. The young couple struggled as did others. The tall, well-built, personable Anthony went to a school, learning English, and applied his education and aptitude to become a New York City fireman. Rose attended the children that came along and was a devoted wife, a fantastic cook, and a woman who made sure that all the daily needs of the family were met.

Every Sunday, the family went together for church services. Working overtime unselfishly was a fundamental part of the immigrant spirit. They had a dream. Everyone worked for it and all shared in the benefits. At the time of his acceptance into the fire department in September 1915, these firemen were still using the strong and serene Percheron horses to pull some of the heavy equipment apparatus. Serving the fire department well, he received commendations and made lifelong friends. Retiring after twenty-five years of exemplary service his records showed that he had saved lives and been hospitalized twice. All through this, he never sought praise or talked about his encounters with deaths.

Undoubtedly, Anthony was humble! They had three children: Josephine, followed two years later by Vito, and an earlier child, a daughter, passed away as an infant. After renting in Manhattan and scrimping and saving for six years, they were able to put a down payment on that ideal home in Brooklyn.

Living there until twenty-two, Vito left about a year after Josephine and her Scottish husband moved in to live with her parents. Raymond was born at King's County Hospital two months after their arrival. Money was tight for the Mastersons since that was the time Sean had just gone out on his own as a printer. Business took time to develop, and with a child was on the way, every penny counted. Living with the Di Mario family helped make ends meet. Many Italian families followed that formula, and some still do today.

His nephew, Raymond, would also recall this home as the place where he spent his childhood, growing to adulthood, and Vito's visiting was an integral part of it. When the youngster took his first steps Vito applauded the loudest. And through the years, countless gifts were placed in this young child's eager hands by his loving uncle. Vito never had children and his bond with the youngster was close and long lasting.

A unique game was played between Vito and his nephew. Anytime he entered the front door on a visit, his shout was always the same: "Have no fear. Your uncle is here!" It didn't take but a second or so for the call to be swiftly answered. No matter where the little guy was in the house, he would come running upstairs or downstairs at full speed to find Vito, leaping into his arms while giving him a child's as-wide-as-possible Olympic gold medal hug, which was fully returned. Unfortunately, for the relative's peace of mind, they knew that this generous, warm, loving, family man had a dark side. When young, he had taken a wrong turn on the road of life, joined the Mafia, eventually advancing to the top.

Anthony had serious talks with his son about right and wrong, but they ended in failure. Vito's passion for the underworld was unstoppable. Sadly, he would not listen. This unacceptable lifestyle brought great pain to those church-going people, but they never lost hope that someday this family member would have a change of heart, finally returning him to the right path.

Through the years, this caused a worried Josephine to lecture her adolescent son not to become involved with her brother in any business dealings, go anywhere with him without permission, or associate with any of Vito's close friends living in the neighborhood. She didn't want her son to have any reason to fall into the deceptive trap of finding the underworld glamourous or as an easy way to make a living. Although it was difficult for her to believe that Vito would intentionally lure Raymond into his way of life, she could not take a chance of there even being a remote possibility! Her son had to find his own respectable path in life, whatever it might be.

When his mother gave reminders, emotions were never a part of the warnings. They were always on point, but deep down, the talks broke her heart. She knew how much Vito loved her son in a genuine way. Eventually, as time passed, Raymond found out the reasons for his mother's concern on his own. The streets talked! However, this realization never changed his feeling toward Uncle Vito. There was only one Vito, and he loved him!

As Raymond reached manhood, one of his mother's gifts, the virtue of honesty, would serve him well. Honesty and objectivity were the founding blocks on which he tried to grow. Back at the restaurant, Vito's time of reminiscing was interrupted by the maître d'. "Mr. Vito, you have a phone call." The pensive mafioso closed his mind to the past, rubbed one large hand against the knuckles of the other, then relocated to his private office upstairs. For these clandestine calls, Vito wasn't ordering food for the restaurant.

CHAPTER 2
The Early Years

Anthony and Rose also proudly owned a ten-acre farm in Vineland, New Jersey, where, from a young age, Raymond spent a good part of each pleasant summer away from the city. The grandparent's house encompassed an acre of land while the other property was leased to a local farmer who grew a variety of produce. New Jersey has a valid reason to be called the Garden State. Vineland's birth is a fairy tale story. The year was 1861, when Philadelphian, Charles K. Landis, a twenty-eight-year-old lawyer, received a five-hundred-dollar gift from his mother. Boldly, he purchased twenty thousand acres in the wilds of southern New Jersey. His dream was that this location would evolve into an epicenter of great thinkers, writers, entrepreneurs, as well as farmers and grape growers, hence, the name Vineland.

Flatbush was so different from the southern Jersey countryside in the 1940s. There, the boy saw horses, cattle, fields of crops, woodlands, and fruit orchards. Fruits and vegetables were picked daily and eaten that same day, which gave them maximum flavor. The air carried the different scents that only the farmland had to offer. To be there challenged any visual or written description of the setting. Nature abounded and touched all the senses.

Outside the house was a large wooden swing hanging from the ceiling of the fully screened porch of the farmhouse. That convenient location for a swing allowed fun for the boy, regardless of the weather. The two-level, three-bedroom farmhouse with its damp cement basement had probably been built in the early 1900s. During that era, in most country homes, the bathroom was also called the outhouse, a new experience for a kid from Brooklyn. It was hard for Raymond to figure out why the people in southern New Jersey had a funny accent when they spoke compared to his family and neighbors back home. Why did school teach people to speak that way?

Perhaps the highlight of the youngster's excitement came into play when Vito visited the country house, arriving in his car, a 1939 black Plymouth Roadster with a rumble seat. He made sure that his nephew and father got the thrill of riding in the open back compartment. Rarely did Raymond have the pleasure of having cool air blow across his body at forty miles an hour or be outside, watching unobstructed trees fly by him.

On the other hand, Anthony, the fireman, knew all well of both pleasant breezes and freezing winter winds blowing across his body as he rode on the open firetruck. Sometimes, the scent of smoke from Vito's cigar, escaping through the driver's window, was also part of the experience. The young boy would cover his nose. Raymond's request was always the same on the way home: "Could we go some more?" Buildings in the city were close together, but this was spacious farmland. There was only one small grocery store that called home on this rural, quiet two-lane countryside roadway, East Landis Avenue. The ride from his family's farmhouse was about five miles before reaching the town of Vineland, and the driver might not see another vehicle moving in either direction during the entire trip.

While riding about with his grandparents, they would occasionally stop the car so that their grandson could fully appreciate all the aspects of country living, now and again pointing out a house or farm where a relative lived. These family connections in Vineland had been the motivation for Anthony and Rose to purchase their property. One noon, they parked on the side of the road to watch a herd of carefree Holstein cows grazing. His grandfather explained that the udders released the fresh milk that the boy drank. Raymond was intrigued, thought about the process for a moment, and became puzzled. "I see where the milk comes out, Grandpa, but how does it get in?"

Telling that story many times in the following weeks, Anthony and Rose proudly laughed with the new listeners each time. During one of his visits, Raymond was at the tender age of five, a memorable event took place, one he would never, never forget. It clearly defined a major difference between the big city and country living and forever placed it in his mind—the fine line between life and death as far as a boy's mind could grasp. Through the years, his understanding of its magnitude matured.

When the last rays of daytime came down darkness dominated, bringing a violent, noisy, lightning-laden thunderstorm into the area. During the downpour, around bedtime, Grandma took him into the small kitchen, which housed, among other things, a real icebox containing one large crystal-clear block of ice at the bottom. Walking past that modern refrigerator, she headed him over to an old white enameled sink, glazed brown on the outside, which sat against a wall. It was time to wash his hands and face, an innate habit of grandmothers.

Not being able to reach the sink top by himself, Rose raised her grandson's body comfortably against the sink's rolled rim. At the same time, she warned, "For now, you better take your hands away from the faucet. The water pipes here are above ground." The blue-eyed, curly brown-haired youngster really didn't understand why that was told to him but quickly obeyed, withdrawing his arms, while he was pulled inches away from the sink. When Grandma turned on the water knob— a loud Bam! Slam! was the result. A bright, fiery blue-and-white flash of lightning shot out the faucet, plummeting directly down into the sink!

The surprised child could not have been more than a foot away from the threatening, high voltage electrical charge, which had traveled through the exposed water pipes and directly into the farmhouse kitchen! This unexpected surge of uncontrolled power caused shouting and created confusion in both. Raymond was startled, but Grandma reacted quickly with warm hugs and kisses, which let him know that he was safe!

This life-and-death drama took less than a second, so fast that neither had time to realize what was taking place. They were frozen in space with no place to retreat! It was a close call, a certain call to eternity, but God was watching over them. This wasn't their time to die! There was a long, active road of life in front of them, but this event placed in Raymond's subconscious mind some sense of fatal danger. There will be other future unexpected happenings in this young man's life in which Raymond will have God, who never sent a bill, working overtime!

As the lad grew older, he was allowed to roam by himself or play with visiting friends on all the family acreage. On the far west end of that property was a white three-board-high wooden fence that divided his grandparent's land from the sprawling two hundred fifty-hundred-acre working farm that ran alongside. In addition to their numerous farming activities, this neighboring spread, the Corsia farm, had a small Thoroughbred breeding operation—one stallion named Lucky Penny, a band of ten broodmares, along with foals and yearlings. Raymond enjoyed leaning or sitting on the fence, watching the mares with their foal graze or frolic about in the tall-grass rich field. On a windy day, this grass swayed, resembling a seamless wave moving across the ocean.

In another field, the yearlings nipped at each other, whinnied, and ran together, occasionally leaping into the air as they threw their hindquarters sideway. They were free spirits. Sometimes an older, friendly mare would bring herself with a foal right up to the place where the Brooklynite was standing so that her head could be softly rubbed. Curiously, the foal watched. For a young city boy who had only petted house dogs or cats, this was a most unique experience. Here in the spacious outdoors, a magnificent Thoroughbred wanted to be his friend.

It was mesmerizing for Raymond to do no more than stand still, watching the Thoroughbreds frolic or graze in their playground. They were beautifully unique. Somehow, being totally engulfed by the fresh air while watching their movements, his young spirit was allowed to share with them an amazing sense of freedom and nature.

At age seven, another significant, life-changing event happened, impinging the youngster's future development. Starting school was on the agenda, and naturally, he was curious to find out what education was all about. In those days, kindergarten attendance was rare; therefore, all newcomers had basically the same starting place. Few, if any, had a preplanned, expensive advantage. Grandma's sister, his aunt Marie, who also lived in the house with her husband, George, told Raymond's parents that a neighboring parish had a better-rated educational program than their own. On that suggestion, his parents enrolled him in that system, thereby changing the location of his primary education, his classmates, and his entire life! How could such a seemingly insignificant event become so dramatic?

The monthly tuition at that educational center was twenty dollars a month for an out-of-parish student to attend. Can you believe that in today's age, a parochial school for twenty bucks a month while those in the parish paid zero. Where have all the dedicated, charitable nuns, who made that financial structure possible, gone?

One of his classmates, George, who lived near him, became his best friend in grade school. However, after graduating, they attended different high schools, not seeing each other for several years. They, by chance, were again reunited as freshmen at St. John's University. By then, both boys had cars and quickly renewed their bond of friendship. One of their favorite evening pastimes was to socialize and play shuffleboard in a pub called, Hayes, located at Ocean Avenue in Flatbush. Nothing else in this area came close to the old-fashioned appeal of the nostalgic structure. This roadhouse built sometime in the late 1800s had a large, covered wraparound wooden front porch that extended eight feet from the building with ample space for chairs to accommodate the waiting travelers while they talked, daydreamed, smoked a cigarette or read the newspaper. A few may have dozed off. Having been an active stagecoach stop in its early days, it uniquely retained the charm of the Old West. With just a little imagination, a romantic person could still see people sitting on the inviting porch, eager to hear the hoof-beat rhythm of the arriving team of carriage horses anxious to reach their destination. Oats, hay, and water would be their rewards.

Inside the pub, there was a long bar with a wall-length polished mirror behind it, a small room off to the back that held six tables, and a dance floor with a jukebox in the corner. Multiple windows filled the narrow room to the front, which housed the old shuffleboard table on which all that room's lighting was centered. There was always an active mix of friendly college guys and gals there on any given night at Hayes. Could you desire more entertainment at eighteen? Had Raymond put as much time and effort into his education as on shuffleboard and social enjoyment, he no doubt would have been an A student. During this part of the college boys' lives, the compulsory military draft hung over them.

According to George, there was an option for them to consider. The Navy offered a program for college students, who, as freshmen, could join the Naval Reserve at Floyd Bennett Field, Brooklyn. This Naval Air Station was located at the ending of the Flatbush Avenue extension, right before the Marine Park Bridge—now called the Gil Hodges Memorial Bridge in honor of the respected, popular, and talented Brooklyn Dodgers' first baseman. What young Brooklyn fellow in those days didn't have Dodgers' blood flowing through his veins? Even the mention of the New York Yankees or the New York Giants could start an argument without any foreseeable end. This military initiative, presented by the US Navy, required that, during the first two years of college, the future candidate attended one weekend a month of active reserve duty with two weeks of training during the summer.

After this stipulation had been completed, they could take a test, if so inclined, to become a Navy pilot. However, at that point, the applicant was going to be activated either into the pilot program or as an enlisted man with two years of active duty, followed by two more years of reserve obligation. When the time came, both took the test but had not realized how many others, including college graduates, would be applying for the limited peacetime enrollment program. They didn't get accepted therefore, becoming enlisted personnel was an unexpected reality. Discontinuing college prematurely and not getting a commission affected the direction of Raymond's life choices and later options.

Although only seven, when sent to the out of parish school were the wheels to his future life turning? Late afternoon, two weeks before his Navy physical checkup, he drove for half an hour by himself to Bergen Beach in Brooklyn to go horseback riding. Arriving at Bar R Stable, a completely wooden structure that boarded twenty riding horses, the handler in charge was sought out. Together, they selected the animal that would be ridden after which, ten bucks were paid for one hour's time on the trail. Upon saddling up, the mount was guided along a dusty cement road, which ended as it passed under a bridge that held the massive six-lane Belt Parkway highway high above. Rider and horse were soon on the quite sandy trail, no one else was out riding at that time.

Three lanes of the highway headed east to Long Island and Montauk Point while those on the opposite side were pointed west to the entrance of the Battery Tunnel, the longest continuous underwater vehicular way in North America. After driving a few minutes through that tunnel passage, which runs directly below the East River, a driver entered the edge of New York City, called the Battery.

The horse path, which ran parallel to the easterly direction of the Belt Parkway, was in the middle of about one hundred yards of beach sand that was spotted with high American grass The outer perimeter of the area eventually touched the muddy water of nearby Rockaway Inlet. The environment was unique and peaceful. Cars' noises and lights quickly faded into oblivion. This rider, alone at twilight time, mounted on a horse with the earth beneath him, felt no attachment to everyday material goods. Raymond experienced a momentary surreal sense of isolation, oneness within himself. Who needed to be distracted by vain conversations or to be involved with any confusions that are part of the everyday world?

Perhaps some lines taken from a poem of the romantic English poet, Shelly, were in his frame of mind at this moment and give meaning to this unique setting "When I have fears that I may cease to be; of the wide world I stand alone and think, till love and fame to nothingness do sink."

Was this deep philosophical thought in the mind of our rider? Yes, but not for long. His gut feelings took over and had him thinking that he was John Wayne, riding by himself, trailing after bandits who had recently robbed a stagecoach! The only pieces of this enchanted world missing were a pistol, rifle, and the bad guys!

As his dark bay, one -thousand- pound animal started galloping along after the outlaws in the uneven sand, it suddenly fell, rolling over him. Luckily, his feet slipped out of the stirrups, sparing him from a serious injury, but he had to protect himself from several wild kicks thrown from the steed as it got up. What happened here was a common scene in Western movies, horse and rider go down, but the animal lifts itself up immediately, not so for the rider! The mile trek back to the stable was lonely, no one to talk with.

Upon finally reaching the barn Raymond was confronted by an angry the stable manager. What happened to my horse? That was his only concern. Such is life! As he undressed that night to take a shower, a ton of sand spilled from his pockets onto the bathroom floor, a reminder of his recent encounter. When the recruit reported, shortly thereafter, for the Navy induction examination, X-rays showed a recently broken rib. Raymond knew that there was something not right after the fall, but it hadn't hurt enough to see a physician. Youth, what a blessing!

CHAPTER 3
The Military

Sooner than later, the active tour of duty became a reality, a new experience for the airdale. He sailed the oceans on an aircraft carrier, "The Intrepid", one of twenty- four Essex class Carriers built during WW Two. It's itinerary, while he was on board for a Mediterranean Cruise, included ports of call in the following countries, Italy, France, Spain, Greece and the Rock of Gibraltar. When the fighter squadron was not at sea it was based at the Naval air station located in Oceana, Virginia.

In June of 1958 he, and fighter squadron, VF33, were at Guantanamo Bay, Cuba, for gunnery practice when an international incident occurred. Several days after the squadron had arrived, a group of sailors, including Raymond, marines, and civilians, returned at 7:30 p.m. by military bus from liberty in Havana. Although the old gray bus had seen numerous back-and-forth trips, it held the bumpy road well.

The atmosphere of the passengers was relaxed, quiet. This group was ready to get back to base, hit the barracks, turn in, and sleep soundly until revelry. They were wiped out; snores were one of the few background sounds heard inside the darkened bus. Next to him sat his squadron buddy, Lou Carmello, a fine fellow from the Bronx. His only fault was being a Giant fan. Without a care in the world, they spoke casually to each other in low tones.

The trip had been underway for several hours when bright headlights appeared in front of them. As the bus stopped, those who were fully awake strained their eyes to see why. They had not hit anything, and there were certainly no red lights on this road. The time of uncertainty was clearly eliminated when three armed soldiers entered the front door while a large contingency of weapon carrying troops quickly surrounded the vehicle! The bus driver opened the sliding door and scrammed! The head of the three-man boarding party spoke immediately and authoritatively declared, "I am Raul Castro. These soldiers are part of the Cuban revolutionary force, and you are our guests. I must ask you to immediately leave the bus now in single file from the front!" The passengers, twenty-four military and twenty-six civilians, had no choice but to comply. At first, those who slept wondered if they were having a bad dream but woke up to reality damn fast.

The rebels guided them to four open trucks with makeshift wooden benches on the inside perimeters. It was a tight squeeze, but everyone found a seat. Tension was understandably high, and the darkness with the unknown terrain didn't help. Uncertainty ruled supreme! Each group of Americans had their own theories of what was going on. Lou was sure it was for ransom. "How much do you think they are gonna want for our release? My parents barely have twenty-five hundred in the bank and no credit."

Playing the part of a teaser with tongue in cheek, Lou's buddy suggested practical advice, "You better learn to speak Spanish fast." Lou was not at a loss for a comeback, so offered his response in two languages, "Buenos dias, amigo . . . Mi casa es su casa . . . Come to see me." Both chuckled. These sailors were optimistic by nature. What was the worst that could happen to these nineteen-year-old American sailors? Sure, as hell, they weren't going to become Cuban rebels!

After hours of uncomfortable travel on bumpy dirt trails, the trucks that held them as passengers made the former Navy bus seem like a Cadillac. Eventually, the detainees started to pass groups of outposts manned by well-organized rebels in an area completely unknown to them. The destination of this planned detour was a secluded military encampment in the vast Sierra Cristal Mountains. Back at Guantanamo Naval Base, it became apparent that the servicemen were long overdue. After a search, the empty, undamaged bus was found in the early morning of the next day, about thirty miles west from the base.

Meanwhile, as the sun rose in the mountain camp, the captives got a clearer view of their surroundings. Seeing a massive horde of rebels, it was difficult to guess exactly how many were encamped on this large, abandoned farm where all the buildings, barns, and shacks were fully utilized. Makeshift tents, well beyond their sight, were located in the rocky fields. Lean-tos of many varieties, which appeared to have been hastily built, were placed against existing structures. This was not a place to call home! The word temporary was written all over the location. An eyeball survey of the rebels' equipment left much to be desired from a military viewpoint. The jeeps, vehicles, and trucks were used and beat up. No two matched. An aircraft was nonexistent. Likewise, the troops had a wide variety of older weapons, which seemed unorthodox for an army going into a life-and-death battle.

In fact, the hostages had made this reasonably safe gathering of Cuban rebels possible. Their abduction was a clever ploy, a strategic move on Fidel's part, to stop the bombing of this location by the Cuban government's airplanes. This offered the rebel troops safety in that area where Raul now entertained his "guests." The fighters in these mountains had been in chaos for weeks with constant air attacks, desperately needing time to regroup. This tactic, kidnapping the Americans accomplished that goal. It was a major factor in the overall winning momentum of the revolution.

This seemingly ragtag group of soldiers also included females who wore little, if any, makeup, yet they had bodies that were well-toned, and some of these young women had a natural, unpretentious beauty. They didn't need eyelashes, creams, or lipstick to be sexy, and the sailors could have cared less. They delighted to be in the sight of females. A few ladies rather enjoyed it, openly flirting with the American sailors. Girls will be girls! The male Cuban soldiers found it somewhat amusing and normal, but they weren't worried. The women slept with them at night.

One called Lola, had a carnal attraction to the tall, blue-eyed Raymond. She chose to hide her desire for the moment by checking quite often with him to see if he needed anything. The directive of keeping the guests as comfortable and quiet as possible came from Raul Castro, and this female took full advantage of the dictate. The sailor knew little Spanish, and her English vocabulary was less extensive therefore, any interaction consisted of elaborate gestures and simple singular words or phrases. Nevertheless, the Americano openly enjoyed the feminine attention and company of such a Cuban beauty. Why not? A beautiful woman is beautiful under any conditions. An envious, thirty-two-year-old first-class petty officer, Rick Thomas, jokingly made a request to Airman Masterson, "See if she has a sister?"

In a businesslike fashion Raymond stated his terms, "It's going to cost you cash!" There was no hesitation in his jovial acceptance. "Name your price." The other sailors in the immediate area clapped and cheered. "Get me one too," indicating their approval. One opened his wallet and flashed some cash. Although at this point, the guests still did not know the reason why they had been highjacked, they did not feel threatened and were relaxed. The detainees joked, told personal stories, played cards, and threw some balls around while taking these inexplicable circumstances in stride. They were not given any work details. In an odd way, this was a mountain vacation without a hotel or pool, and they were still on the US government payroll.

Washing facilities and bathrooms were sparsely located at different places since this was a makeshift camp. The quasi-designated latrine areas consisted of multiple poorly put together, half-covered outhouses hastily built and unisex. If it was raining, best try to find something to cover your head. The nearest to the American group took about three minutes to walk from that area through a narrow, twisting, rocky path hosting trees with underbrush on its side to reach the restrooms.

It was dusk when Raymond returned from nature's call. Suddenly, Lola appeared. If this little hottie was so inclined to sing a song at this time, the lyrics would have been, "Whatever Lola wants, Lola gets." The fixed captive set his eyes on her! Carefully looking around, she heard no one, saw no one, and glided downhill toward Raymond. Stopping before the sailor, Lola pressed her breasts firmly on his chest, then gently rubbed them against him. The surprised, shocked sailor raised his hands placing them squarely on Lola's shoulders to hold her steady, slowing her down while buying time to figure out his next move. Did he want to have sex with Lola or better asked, would that be a smart decision or not? It would be pleasurable for sure, but would a yes be well advised? The nineteen-year-old, in a general sense, was her prisoner.

The female Cuban didn't know exactly how to interpret Raymond's physical grasp on her. Lola expected this man's hands to be tight on her hips, squeezing her warm body closer, not tightly on the upper body, restricting any movements. Was this female warrior not enough woman? Backing up, she completely opened her blouse. Nothing covered her braless, luscious, exposed breasts. Perhaps, more sexually suggestive activity needed to take place, so she cupped her breasts in her hands, and generously offered them to him as forbidden fruit. This act fully aroused his sex drive and imagination, but his thought process was still functioning somewhat!

Rushing through his mind was the first possibility: I wish that I was anywhere in the world but here! Why me to have this unbelievable temptation in the middle of nowhere? If this was only a dream, the ending would be a pleasurable certainty! The second possibility: she could have a lot of jealous boyfriends in this rebel army, all with guns and machetes. Not good odds if they came hunting for me. The third possibility: if I shun her cold, she might be angered, and there is no wrath like the wrath of a woman scorned. What if she ran down the path, yelling, "Rape, rape?" Perhaps the last words that I ever heard!

How would she behave? Raymond didn't know her at all as to guess any answer. A wrong move here might be the end of his world. The final corresponding thought connected all the above: a bad decision here and "Bang! Bang!" Adios! There I am, standing before a revolutionary Cuban firing squad! They don't miss! All these premonitions came simultaneously in a flash, but the answer wasn't among them. These were all so negative options! Lust was not represented! Hesitantly, after several serious seconds of soul-searching the other side of the coin, desire had its say. For the past year, he was stationed at the naval military base or on an aircraft carrier. One might rightly say that his passions were starving. All these pros and cons options that involved his feelings came in a flash, but the answer still wasn't among them either.

Opposites dramatically pulled at Raymond who was between the proverbial rock as a revolutionary hostage and the hard place—Lola's warm, soft, curvy body! Every effort was made to be strong, to be noble, but it was futile. His body shook with passion; this strong urge was impossible to walk away from. A thirsty man in a desert doesn't turn his back on a drink of water! The sailor succumbed, taking hold of Lola's soft hand as they disappeared into the thick woods. This was but the first visit of several rendezvous in that romantic setting.

For a long time, the sensual fantasies of Lola in the woods would be there to ignite his imagination. The captives had not been abused. In fact, Raul Castro and his staff repeatedly went out of their way to tell them as he had done on first entering the commandeered bus that they were guests, not hostages. Consideration for their safety and health was always evident. They ate the same food, although not great, as the troops, slept on the same type of mats, and on site there was always a doctor available. No appointment or insurance card was necessary. Prescriptions were free.

The Castro brothers were not currently looking to have a battle with US forces. Kidnapping the Americans was a brazen, desperate move to advance their revolution with grave consequences if it failed! Perhaps they believed that there was nothing to lose, everything to gain!

During this deceptive maneuver, Raul had allowed, better said invited, the press into camp for news releases. It was great public relations for the rebels while also making the Americans feel more secure. Seeing famous reporters from the free world roaming about the grounds eliminated anxiety. Some detainees were interviewed, perhaps it was a chance in a lifetime to have world fame. One of their quotes might be printed.

The rebels eventually released all the hostages, unharmed, but gradually over a three-week period. Navy helicopters were permitted to land at the encampment for the unceremonious evacuations. Raymond was in the last group of ten sent back to Gitmo. He never saw Lola again! This chance for Raymond to spend three weeks closely observing the characteristics of a young Raul, Castro's brother, and a future prime minister of Cuba along with the rebels was more than unique! Albeit terribly tragic, this time frame was history in the making.

Lola, well, she was something else! The Cuban senorita would never be found in history books; however, her beauty, qualities, and the memories that she created were timeless!

CHAPTER 4
Another World—High Society

In another part of the world an extremely wealthy family's daughter attended a private girl's boarding high school academy. It was located on over one hundred acres of prime land intertwined and surrounded by woodlands and trails, in the picturesque town of Hampton Bays, Long Island. On the outside property could be found a heated swimming pool, ten tennis courts along with two regulation-size soccer fields. A fully staffed stable with above sleeping quarters for the manager kept ten fine riding horses available to be ridden after classes. It took a rainy day to keep them in their stalls.

A driving range and a nine-hole putting green satisfied those interested in golf. An inside gym housed another pool, two basketball courts, and enough gymnastic equipment to please anyone preparing for athletic competition. Activities during the week trickled to a standstill at the weekends, for most of the young socialites were at home or visiting the families of their classmates. This academic institution had a worldwide reputation regarding scholastic achievement and social status.

Several days after her graduation from this prestigious establishment, her parents, Charles, and Isabel Brockhurst, asked their daughter Suzanne to join them in the mansion library located on the second floor of their Old Westbury estate for a family talk. It was not the first time such a get-together was called, but Suzanne hadn't a clue what this was about.

Well known in the elite business, social, and philanthropic circles of New York, the Brockhursts were conscious of their status and responsibilities, that led them to continually instill those qualities into their only child's life. Charles and Isabel believed they had thought of another way for their daughter to continue developing her senses of empathy along with responsibility so that she would follow the high standards of their family traditions, which had guided their every move.

One of their favorite charities was the Sisters of Mercy Home for destitute women located in Lafayette, Louisiana. They wanted Suzanne to agree with them to spend the next two months, her summer break before university, at that institution. Their hope was that their newly graduated daughter would learn firsthand that which the unfortunate experienced along with the effort, time. and expenses involved in caring for these castaways. It was a practical chance to see financial hardship, illness, and loneliness. This experience should give her a broader view of life.

They believed that Suzanne needed to see both sides of life! It was realistically presented as a great challenge, but at first, the young lady was uncertain whether she could handle such an ordeal or even wanted to travel. She answered that time was needed to think it over. Her parent understood the on- the- spot dilemma, suggesting that their loved one should take a day or so, making her own decision with no need to feel guilty if the answer was no.

Pondering the pros and the cons, her heart believed that the parents were certain about this fantastic character-building opportunity for a young woman. Yet giving up frequent summer visits as a house guest of friends who lived in Southampton beach was no easy choice. She would not have her new sports car, a Mercedes-Benz 300 SL roadster convertible to drive or be able to enjoy the fantastic Atlantic Ocean beaches. How many gala social events would she miss while in Louisiana? Her friend in Old Westbury would be far away for what would seem like forever. What to do?

Finally, after juggling all the negative and positive thoughts for the best part of a day, the answer was a yes. She was determined to give the plan her all. Previous phone conversations by her parents with the Mother Superior had already gained approval for the summer internship, so it was just a question of packing a few suitcases and buying a round trip first-class ticket on Delta Airlines.

Upon arriving, she found a spacious three-story late-1800 Victorian stone building in muted colors with towers and dormers. A wide wrap around porch with decorative railings was visible on two sides. This large, refurbished structure held twenty-four rooms, each housing two women at the same time. Living spaces that accommodated twelve nuns with their helpers, who shared three to a room, had been added as a wing. It was a far cry from what she called home. The residency was big, but it did not qualify for her as she knew an elaborate mansion to be, nor did it have any maids or butlers. This edifice was functional however, grandeur was not part of its equation.

Her parents were correct. This experience would give her a new outlook on life. As they must, the nuns had everything on a tight schedule, which everyone was expected to follow. It was up at 5:00 a.m., Mass at 5:45 a.m., breakfast at 6:30 a.m., and then on to the day's work, sharply at 7:30 a.m., and ending usually before 7:00 p.m., when a skeleton night crew took over. By that time, there wasn't much left to do, nor did any day workers have the energy to do it. Some helpers were assigned to be the aid of a specific nun. This inexperienced Long Island novice was to be at the side of a dedicated nun

Sister Joan Matie was a tall, slender, personable, soft-spoken twenty-six-year-old native of Broussard, Louisiana. For these ladies, the workdays blended together with the basic needs of the cared-for women as the priority. If the boarders could not bathe themselves, they were helped, meals were cooked and served to them while those who required medical attention were treated. Dialog and counseling abounded. The ladies that were taken into the house were starving for conversation and friendship as much as for spiritual, physical, and material needs.

The responsibilities of an aide covered all those avenues except medication. Only the trained sisters could perform medical treatments for the women. The young woman from Long Island did herself proud, for she carried out all tasks without a complaint and with complete willingness. She and the saintly sister were perfectly matched, forming a bond. On one occasion, this humble nun was cleaning and bandaging a nasty wound on a formerly homeless woman's thigh, which had been grossly neglected before she came to them. There was a putrid smell around a three-inch square area that was covered with proud flesh, where normal granulation tissue had gone wild.

Awkwardly, conscientiously, Suzanne backed away from Sister Joan Matie as the nun started to care for this poor soul. Expressing her sensual uneasiness, she confessed, "I couldn't do that for all the money in the world." Gently, Sister Joan Matie raised her head away from the ugly wound and with a faint, gentile smile gave words of deep spiritual inspiration, "Neither could I."

It was a moment that Suzanne Brockhurst would never, ever forget. She learned forever that money had its place and, sometimes, no place. Her parents wanted their daughter to mature, and in that special second of unselfish love shown by Sister Matie, Suzanne made a giant leap in that direction.

In late August, Suzanne returned home from that summer experience. All sights were now focused on starting at Harvard, University located in Cambridge, Massachusetts. The selected major would be in finance, and upon graduation, joining the family's business empire was inevitable. There would be no interview requirement, and one day, she would be the chairwoman with a Harvard degree and the Brockhurst wealth. The whole world laid at her feet! If the term, red carpet ever needed a setting, this was it. The parents were well-pleased that Suzanne had accepted their unusual challenge, which she herself objectively saw as a successful character builder and a chance to be touched by the hard realities of life without experiencing any of the underlying pains. However, one thing was for sure, this lady had no desire of becoming a nun! She knew that the right man was somewhere in her distant future.

Concentrating then on her education, the parents wanted everything to be perfect. Consequently, they purchased a two-bedroom apartment not far from the sprawling campus. That setup would make occasional visits comfortable for them and a sensible way to be sure that all her needs were met, including privacy, with ample space to invite guests to spend time there when she wished. Her new sports car, which had been garaged for two months, was ready to show mileage on the odometer. Besides being intelligent and social, she always involved herself in school activities. On the list of the extracurricular activities at Harvard was the self-funded equestrian club, which she immediately joined, a natural choice since she was riding and jumping horses since eight. A drawer full of ribbons proved her talent.

One of the others to sign up was Luca Tarantino, a nineteen- year- old freshman exchange student, from Southern Italy. Tall, handsome, and articulate, this accomplished horseman spoke three languages fluently. Although he never talked about his home, it was obvious that in his background could be found a wealthy, somehow influential family. He carried himself with dignity, dressed well, and the first time he dated Suzanne, she was in for a surprise. When they reached his black Cadillac Deville, he opened the backdoor, which puzzled her. Why wasn't she going to sit up front with him? Quickly, the lady realized that a chauffeur sat behind the wheel. "Oh, you have a driver." "Yes, he is my cousin, Gino."

Once both were sitting comfortably together inside, Luca introduced her to the driver. "Suzanne, this is my first cousin, Gino Tarantino. He is working for my family's import business while staying with me. He also takes me wherever I need to go." Half-turning sideways, Gino presented a huge, authentic smile along with a short "Hello, lady" greeting. "How special. A chauffeur. Why didn't my father think on that?" was Suzanne's reaction. "I must apologize. Gino understands only fundamental English, so when speaking with him, our conversation will be in Italian." "As long as you don't talk about this lady, it will be fine." "It is a promise . . . Never!"

They continued to date, taking advantage of visiting the cultural centers and sporting events held in that metropolitan city. They were two young people without seemingly a care in the world, enjoying each other's company, having fun. Their physical good looks blended well, occasionally turning heads as they passed by others. What happened at certain restaurants in the Italian section of Boston amused her curiosity. Luca didn't get a bill while the last words of the proprietors were, "I hope you and the signorina enjoyed your meals. Please come back soon."

The first time it occurred, Suzanne inquired, "Why didn't they charge you?" With a twinkle in his dark brown eyes, he answered, "Only in A-ME-RI-CA, they love me!" The foreigner could not help but burst out laughing. The inquisitive Long Islander tried again. There had to be a better answer. "Stop joking."

This time the response was more acceptable. "These fine people know my family in Italy. They would not insult them by taking my money." It amazed his date that Luca's family was known halfway around the world. She had been introduced to important people through her parents, but were any of them more internationally known than her boyfriend?

On a freezing evening in January, after returning from Christmas break, Luca and Suzanne were eating in one of his favorite Italian places, the cozy "Celeste Palazzo di Vincenzo" As the continental meal ended, he unexpectedly expressed to her a wish, "I am in the mood to do a little gambling." He might as well had told his date that he wanted to go to the moon. She had no idea what he was talking about.

"What? Where?"

"Follow me." He took her by the hand as they walked down a darkened hallway, which passed alongside an active kitchen until reaching a large sliding metal door. A courteous man stood there to open it, and behind that entrance was another slightly smaller wooden door which he also opened. The view immediately changed from a bustling kitchen setting to a gambling room with a dozen or more players in action. Into her sight came two blackjack tables, a dice table, and a roulette wheel. Suzanne felt like her favorite childhood character, Alice, who was unexpectedly swept down the rabbit's hole into a brand-new wonderland! Nervously, she whispered into Luca's ear, "Can we get into trouble? This looks illegal."

In his easy Italian manner, he assured her that this room was as old as the restaurant. "Nothing to worry about, dear. Enjoy. Everybody here is a friend. It is a social pastime." Sitting his date at a blackjack table, Luca stood behind her as the dealer changed his five hundred dollars into twenty red chips. Luca seemed knowledgeable at that game, but it was no comfort to Suzanne, who was still nervous with good reason. The thought of jail was unthinkable! Mom and Dad would die!

After half an hour of playing, a dreaded sound was heard. The doors were unceremoniously thrown open. It was a police raid! The olive-skinned Italian turned pale but reacted immediately. He grabbed Suzanne by the arm pulling her to follow him. The police whistles blew, and there was yelling around them. This circumstance left no time for questions or answers! Luca grabbed her hand and darted for a narrow corridor at the corner of the gambling room, which led to the restrooms. It was into the men's room where he jumped up onto the white double sink unit and lifted Suzanne up to be at his side. Closely above them was a window which he opened, pushing Suzanne through the darkened space so that they could escape. He was right behind her, and soon, both were in a poorly lighted alley. So far, the effort was successful. Luckily, the police had failed to surround the building.

Once reaching the street, at Luca's request, the pair nonchalantly walked, hand in hand, in a direction away from the restaurant's entrance. Suzanne's heartbeat was at full throttle; her long, sexy, well-defined legs were numb. She forced herself to ask, "Are we out of trouble?" The Italian coolly responded, "I sure hope so. Keep walking . . . Smile and don't dare to look back. Please give me a kiss or two. That should make us appear to be lovers out for a walk." In no time, the black Deville pulled alongside them and Luca guided his date inside. This exciting evening was over! They both were physically and emotionally exhausted and decided that taking Suzanne back to her apartment was the best way of calling it a night. This was not the type of secret that she could keep from her parents. The top priority next morning was to call home! Somehow, since it turned out alright, Isabel, as a mother, found some humor in the story.

Anyway, she warned her daughter to be more careful, that she might not be as lucky another time, and then casually asked the young man's name and facts about him. That information was quickly relayed to Charles, who had a check run on Luca Tarantino, a nineteen-year-old exchange student from Sicily, Italy, who attended Harvard.

The results showed that he was the second son of Giovanni Tarantino, the godfather of Tutti-Quanti in Palermo, Sicily. Immediately and factually, Charles relayed these findings to his naive daughter with a stern order! "Gangsters and their families are the last people in the world that you want to associate with . . . No way! They always go to jail or get shot. End the relationship fast!"

So, sadly, she did. Luca also realized that dating this lady was, let's say, not in either one's best interest after the gambling incident. The Italian was always keenly aware of who he was and who she was. He still found her beautiful, charming, and would always show respect. Whenever or wherever they crossed paths after the breakup, pleasant hellos and conversation were always comfortably exchanged. They were still friends, would always be friends, and his assistance was offered if ever needed. This thoughtful young man's character naturally conveyed charisma.

Suzanne even learned a few Italian phrases to share with Gino, the bodyguard. Still, she thought the godfather's son was basically a decent guy, smart, lots of fun, and what a looker! Although never thinking about it in this way, suddenly, she had a Mafia connection.

CHAPTER 5
Home Coming

After Raymond's military stint, he returned to regular life: winning at shuffleboard, dates, a summer job, and back to school. Being in the military service, experiencing the world, being involved with outside physical activities, mixing with squadron buddies from different backgrounds and states caused his mind to lean away from the academic environment.

A new switch had been turned on, causing difficulty in settling back into reading books or studying for tests. School bordered on dull. This inability to adjust from military life back to civilian ways was not unique; others experienced the same difficulty. Before the service, he was a B average student; however, after returning from the Navy, his average dropped to a C, which included one D-plus grade. He wanted to earn a degree, but to continue in this manner was not up to his standards. Lacking focus disappointed him. Even though he was aware that this happened to others, he blamed himself. Soon came a tough decision: what's next? Was there a way to beat this obstacle?

Never having set his sights on any specific profession or been naturally inclined to one, this young veteran didn't know how to proceed! Who, when starting in a university at seventeen or eighteen, really knows how he will spend the rest of his life. Aptitude tests gave Raymond a high rating in the areas of outdoors, artistic, and persuasive endeavors. He joked with his friends about this range of vocational possibilities that left him options somewhere between being a forest ranger, another Van Gogh, or be a top salesman and sell the Brooklyn Bridge twice. Great choices but unrealistic! Cutting back on schoolwork made sense, so he

33

enrolled in night school for the next semester, deciding to enter the New York business world. Maybe those changes would turn things around. Graduation would be a little later, but destiny had already figured that in the equation. Regardless, whatever the field, he was the type who ultimately would not just look for a job but a fulfilling vocation. He was willing to become involved in a passionate way with the direction of his life,

Raymond was willing to work hard, taking the best chance on achieving success if the right opportunity could be found. At first, following the line of least resistance, the jobseeker landed a position as a sales representative for a huge New York City company. After several months, it became clear to him that the city and corporate life was not his calling; swimming into that stream wasn't going to happen. A thought came, could there be something wrong with him as everybody else seemed to be able to adjust or naturally blend in? Why couldn't he?

Getting up a six thirty in the morning to shower, shave, down a cup of coffee and toast or either a cold cereal for breakfast before leaving his apartment at seven thirty to catch a crowded bus, boarding a more jammed train, and finally reaching a grossly packed city didn't make sense, at least not for him! Nevertheless, his inquiring young mind never gave up! He started researching, even into the late hours, after school and work for different possibilities that might reward his search for achievement once and for all.

Luckily, one day, a new experience came over to his life and enabled Raymond to see a whole new, marvelous environment. The surroundings spoke of a truly different world—no buses, no trains, no high-rise mausoleums. It was a Saturday afternoon, and there he stood on the ground-level apron area of a Thoroughbred racetrack where people were dressed casually. They came out for a day of action, perhaps lucky enough to cash a few tickets. This area and the crowd around him were in stark contrast to the exclusive, well-dressed box area patrons on the upper second tier.

He was invited to the races by two of his workplace friends, Artie and Kevin, the only reason for the outing. The fellows in their twenties leisurely walked around the paddock where the horses were being saddled. Enthusiastic people passed them from several directions adding to the sense of activity. This was Raymond's first time at a horse track, and it was exciting. After studying the changing, flashing odds listed for the first race, he asked his friend, "Artie, who wins more, you or Kevin?"

Eagerly, Artie replied, "Follow my picks, and you will be a millionaire!" Kevin couldn't wait to chime in, "Yeah, Artie, you would have Ray a million in the hole by the third race."

Not offended by that remark, Artie was still willing to be an adviser, "Hey, Ray, let me know when you are ready to place a wager. Bet a few bucks and you own the horse for the whole race!" Enthused by the endless movement around them, he declined. Raymond's big smile showed the enjoyment he experienced. "This place is great! I want to soak up the surroundings instead. You two make a score, fill your pockets." Continuing to key in, the spectacle entranced him. Raymond saw a masterpiece in the synchronized motion of the horses, the jockeys, the vibrant people, and each race as it was run. The announcer's appealing voice brought all the parts together.

Deep inside, this unique thrill had sparked his soul. The adrenalin rush of the players who were moving past him to get their bets down on a sure winner fascinated him. As the crowd vocalized near the finish of a race, yelling for their horse to be first, his heartbeat faster. The passion for this thrill was genuine since he hadn't placed a bet all day.

In the back of his mind, he conjured up those memories of childhood days at the New Jersey farm where he touched Thoroughbred mares and was within feet of their curious foals. Those young horses, when grown, would eventually compete at Thoroughbred racetracks as were the horses in the starting gate on that race card. His friends, always at his side, continued to study their racing charts more in-depth after each event. Out of curiosity, Raymond asked them how things were unfolding. Were they winning or losing? The two players looked at each other, and Kevin gave this profound gambler's answer, "We get better as the day progresses."

An imaginative thought came to Raymond, and before he could stop himself, the idea was expressed to his buddies, "What a way to make a living—racehorses, the outdoors, the beautiful people, nonstop excitement . . . I like it."

Kevin gave the first knock. "Race trackers work seven days a week. Horses eat and train every day regardless of the weather. Do you get it?" "So what?" Raymond countered. "It doesn't matter. Seven days a week of doing what you like, it is way better than one day a week doing what you don't like." Stepping in, Artie reinforced Kevin, "Easy now. You're doing well at the office, working hard and in good standing. Our company will make you a manager in a couple of years. It's a no-brainer. Watch, your salary will take a big jump."

Annoyed with himself for expressing his secret discontentment aloud in the first place, Raymond retorted, "Maybe true, but I'm not sure, that sales or the city are my things. I travel from one stuffy office to another where the people in them seem to want to be somewhere else. Is that all life has to give?"

Wanting the magic answer, Artie dug deeper by asking, "What are people supposed to do? Rob a bank and then retire?" These words inspired the invitee. "Everybody must find their own destiny whatever way possible even it means taking a leap of faith." The last part was echoed back in unison by his buddies with a hint of irony, "A leap of faith?" "You can bet on that, a sure winner. Say a prayer, keep your eyes open, and jump! It's all about trying. A person can't win if they give up. I'm still looking and will never quit!"

This was Kevin's last shot to bring Raymond back to reality. "You know the old folk wisdom. Don't give up your day job . . . while you're looking." They all laughed as Kevin totally had changed the serious matter to a light-hearted joke while pointing to a nearby food stand, "Let's get some hot dogs and a few beers." The other two were ready. They had enough of wasting time debating improbabilities. Raymond picked up the tab at the food counter as a way of showing gratitude to his hosts.

By the day's end, Raymond had visually, emotionally, and mentally absorbed as much as it was possible from this racetrack experience. Upon leaving the course after the ninth race, the newcomer sincerely thanked the guys for suggesting the races. They departed in different directions to find their cars in the track's parking lot and returned home.

Raymond asked himself why he had never gone to the races before? Continuing his position in the city, he could not help but think about how fantastic life in the Thoroughbred world would be. If his mind had a momentary break from the business at hand, horses would flash in his mind. As this obsession grew, a game plan was needed along with some courage to execute it. Finally, the decision was made to go to the races on a Saturday, attempting to speak with some trainers for information and seeking their professional advice. Perhaps the right person to help him was out there.

The first several trainers approached were not overly helpful. They seemed too busy, and suggestions were not on their agendas. It was obvious they did not have the time to be annoyed with someone's wild, impractical dream. All meetings ended with a quick goodbye and a wish of good luck.

Finally, a productive talk evolved with one of them, a dignified old timer in his late sixties who walked with a limp resulting from a World War II injury. However his age, the gentleman kept himself in good shape and dressed meticulously. The old style of the trainer's binoculars with the worn leather straps from which they hung was easily noticeable. That alone told the tale of their age and the numerous races that must have been seen through them. If the binoculars were more closely examined, even a deeper observation would have been forthcoming. An inscription, "Property of the U. S. Government," would have been found on them, for these glasses were issued to Lt. Commander Joseph J. Hardy USN during that war.

The enthused racing fan approached this trainer. "Sir, do you hava minute?" Giving his undivided attention, the trainer said, "Sure. I'm Joe Hardy, and I always have a minute. What's on your mind?" Feeling comfortable from the start in this man's company, Raymond continued, "Mr. Hardy, I'm Raymond Masterson, an outsider who would like to get involved in racing. I think I have a calling to your sport."

The trainer offered a handshake. "Well, well. First, call me Joe. Secondly, do you know anything about the business or anybody in Thoroughbred racing?" After reluctantly shaking his head, came this awkward disappointing response, "To say the truth . . . sorry, nothing and nobody. You are the only one that has time for a conversation."

The old-timer could sense that this man who stood before him was temporarily at a loss for words. Being perceptive and considerate, Joe made it easy. "Tell me then something about yourself." That was the spark Raymond needed. "I'm twenty-four, single, completed three years of college, going to night school, presently working as a sales consultant for a company in the city, and have served in the Navy."

The trainer had achieved his goal; the inquisitive person was now at ease. "Sound credentials. I also served in the Navy, a little before your time. That sort of makes us shipmates." Pausing for a moment, Joe Hardy gave his would-be applicant an intuitive, visual character evaluation. There in front of him stood a fine looking, clean-cut, polite young man with a strong desire in his voice and eyes to get into Thoroughbred racing.

"All right, son, I can give you a chance. You would have to start at the bottom of the ladder as a hot-walker seven days a week at $175. It's the best I could offer you. You begin in a week if you can accept those conditions."

The applicant had no idea what the chores of a hot walker were, but this was not the time for questions. So, he put his hand out to shake Joe's hand, sealing the deal in a thankful manner. "I'm your new hot-walker." Smiling, Joe gave him a compliment, "You know, you are enough of a risk-taker to maybe do something with it in racing. I'll keep an eye on your progress, helping you if possible."

The new employee could not have been happier. "Thanks! Not even a resume. Easiest interview I have ever had!" The trainer made a proud confession, "Never read one. Don't want to read one either. Kind of a waste of time. I'm a believer in face-to-face relationships and conversation."

Both men laughed, parted, and went on their ways, Joe to watch his horse run, leaving the hopeful, to be horseman, to dream on. Neither of the two realized how significant this meeting would be to both of their lives. The new hot-walking job started and initiated as well a long long list of questions. Raymond wanted to assure himself that every move he did was the right one! This was not the time to look foolish or, even worse, get fired!

When horses came back from racing or training, they were given a warm soapy bath by their grooms. A hot-walker's first task, Joe informed him, was to hold and control that horse by a shank (a long piece of leather with a chain attached at the end which wrapped securely around the horse's halter. It gave the handler control with no discomfort to the animal). During this refreshing event, a Thoroughbred might be fractious; therefore, the hot-walker or handler had to be alert. With any racehorse, it never took more than a moment for them to injure themselves or hurt someone. A thousand-pound animal with the reflexes of a cat demanded full attention.

Joe told this newcomer to observe the technique for a bit, and then someone would stand by him on his first effort—graduate school. After the excess water had been removed, scrapped off with a smooth-edged, long, thin semi-rounded metal object, the hot walker would walk with the animal for about half an hour or more around the barn shed row until the horse was completely dried. This overall procedure was called cooling out. To place a Thoroughbred back in its stall while still wet could cause an unhealthy result, such as a fever or cough, and that was the last thing any trainer wanted.

During the time that the horse walked around the shed row cooling out, it was allowed only limited amounts of water on each turn. This procedure was followed so that the animal did not drink too much water quickly and become prone to developing colic. Since he was so attracted to racing, Raymond did extra work helping grooms filling water buckets, putting oats in the horse's feed tubes, or whatever. He spent all his spare time in the stalls, watching the grooms work and holding bandages, liniments, safety pins, and fetching all they needed. It became the new guy's self-assigned tasks.

Their patience was tested by the thousands of questions he asked, but they felt important about being able to help a newcomer. Not too many people asked grooms for knowledge. Eventually, he benefited from the groom's instructions to the point where, at times they watched, allowing him in his spare time to do their work. They saw that he was anxious to learn. With an easy way about himself, he was accepted and liked by his fellow stable workers, some of whom were not even high school graduates. Very often, they were seen in conversation and laughed together.

One morning, Raymond knelt on his right knee, placing a bandage on a horse's leg. The groom observed patiently, but his face showed distress and worry. Confiding to his freelance helper, the man said, "I have to go back to Mexico . . . Immigration problems." Immediately standing from his kneeling position, he gave the perplexed persons his complete attention. "Sorry, to hear that, Andre. When do you have to leave?" "I have two weeks to return home or else."

"That's sad. It's tough enough to be so far away from your family while you are supporting them, and now, you are being stopped Speaking softly, Andres disclosed his despair, "It is lonely here. My wife and three children mean everything to me, and now this. I don't even have enough money to make home. Each week, most of my pay goes back to them." Putting his right hand on the groom's shoulder to comfort him, Raymond then reached into his back pocket. Taking out his wallet he drew out six wrinkled twenty-dollar bills which were carefully, discretely placed on Andre's palm. With sincerity, Raymond stated, "This will help a little with your trip home, and I will keep you and your family in my prayers." The groom was overwhelmed. Taking Raymond's hand between his, he pressed it then expressed a warm, "Gracias, señor. Dios te bendiga."

CHAPTER 6
A Groom

Reaching Joe's office, Raymond entered finding the trainer sitting behind a large mahogany desk facing a set of comfortable leather executive seats. These quarters had pictures of winning stake horses on the walls, cabinets filled with books. A solid dark brown indoor-outdoor rug covered the floor, and a well-stained coffeemaker sat on a side table. There wasn't any tack or racing supplies in the room, only personal mementos and trophies; reminders of jubilant past victories which now stood on shelves.

The surroundings showed years of thoughtfully being put together and maintained as a business office. The fledgling hot walker expressed himself, "Joe, Andre told me some bad news." The trainer did not act surprised. "Yes, I already know it. Poor fellow. Good family man. This shouldn't be in his life. He deserves better. I'll help with travel expenses and put enough in his pocket to hold him over until he can return. The least I can do. It should give our friend peace of mind."

The critical point that Raymond was hoping to reach arrived. Now for the moment of truth. "Joe, do you think I'm ready to take his place?" There wasn't any hesitation on the listener's part. "Why not? You work hard, you're dependable, and have learned a lot. Sure." The hot walker was relieved. "Joe, thanks for the chance. I'll never let you down."

My least worry: "I'm a good judge of character." In the capacity of a groom, he then washed the Thoroughbreds, brushed, bandaged, fed, and talked to these regal animals with a certain kind of friendship. If they didn't eat everything, he might have asked why or generally questioned them with horse sense if they were feeling okay. He never did get a response. However predictable was the result of those exchanges when patting one of his chargers on the neck, the noble animal felt the warm touch, moving their head closer to Raymond's chest. Now, what counted was that in his usual interaction with the horses, Raymond created a new relation between them. Certainly, it was a type of gift.

He mucked and raked out the stalls then bedded them down carefully with abundant clean golden-yellow straw. The dust was carefully shaken out of the hay before it was placed into a chain hay rack found high off the ground in a catty-corner back part of the stall. He gave the horses liniment massages, groomed them, cleaned out their feet daily, packing them with mud every other day, which helped keep them pliable. A horse with a cracked hoof presented a serious problem.

Saddling them for morning training was part of the routine and giving the exercise rider a leg up was the final touch before his charge left for the training track. Grooms always brought the horses under their care to the paddock for racing. One day, as he walked his horse around the circular ring in the paddock, Raymond caught a glimpse of a beautiful woman.

Appearing to be in her early twenties, she was tall, shapely, with auburn hair that loosely touched her shoulders. Her outfit must have come from the finest boutique that the city had to offer. Raymond encountered perfection! The word beautiful was the simplest way to describe this dream of a woman. Her demeanor, in that setting, near the center of the tree-shaded paddock showed that she had an outgoing personality as she thoroughly enjoyed the company of the other three women with whom she spoke. They seemed never to stop gesturing and smiling, these society ladies showed not a care in the world. They had the world in their hands.

For a short time, she was in his line of vision, but as he moved along with his runner around the walking ring, he lost sight of her. His instincts said to look back, but his better judgment told him that such a glance would be in poor taste, classless, and embarrassing to a true lady. He was only a groom; she was, in his mind, a queen!

On his next turn around the paddock, by chance, she turned, looking over in his direction. Their eyes met. It was only for a split moment, but both sensed an attraction without any chance of continuance. How many encounters of that nature never went a step further only to become lost down memory lane? Nevertheless, this good-looking- young man had managed to capture her attention. Has not every person felt that fleeting experience of momentary love at least once in their life?

The riders then waited for the riders up call. Shortly thereafter, the field was headed to the racetrack while the bettors surrounding the paddock area began dispersing. All the parties in the paddock disappeared to the box area, and soon, that area was completely empty. The curtain had gone down on that stage. Although Raymond watched his horse warm up before the race, his thoughts were fixed somewhere else. What a woman! Unfortunately, there wasn't any way for it to be more than a fleeting fascination.

For the next ten months, the new groom did all that was asked of him and more. Although Joe was busy in his office, when he saw Raymond pass by, he called him inside. "Ray, come in. I have something on my mind." The invitee entered, quickly resting on one of the leather seats. Putting his paperwork aside, the trainer expressed an observation, "Son, you have come a long way in slightly over a year. You have a natural talent around horses and have done exceptionally well in a fairly short period by racetrack standards."

"I've been watching and learning. You're, a patient teacher," was his thoughtful answer. "Your crew has let me work with them, they taught me. It all adds up, helping me develop." Then going right to the heart of the matter, for Joe was not one for wasting time, he said, "I have a proposal. My assistant trainer is leaving, going out on his own, perhaps prematurely. His job is open, and I feel confident offering that position to you." The response was immediate. "Thank you. I'm ready!" The only detail offered by the trainer was "Now you make $500 a week." "What am I going to do with all that extra money? Getting up at four thirty in the morning doesn't give me much chance to have any wild nights in the city."

The answer was very simple but pointed, "Save it for rainy days. They are certain in this business." Those words came from years of experience. The ups and downs are integral parts of Thoroughbred racing. Each horseman had to cope, and some will disappear. The new assistant expressed hope, "Maybe I'll stay lucky. Luck has been with me so far.

Things are moving fast." "I don't think I've seen anyone ever advanced quicker than you have, but there is always the exception."

Naturally adept at directing the barn operations, Raymond forged the training hours together smoothly. For starters, every morning, he stopped in front of each Thoroughbred's stall for a visual inspection of the horse, listening to any observations noted by the groom. His eyes were always on the lookout for new physical dangers that might be present near or in that space. Horsemen must constantly be alert to protect their charges. There is no telling the number of Thoroughbreds that are hurt by avoidable circumstances.

The assistant directed the grooms as to which horses they should have ready for a given set. He pointed the exercise riders to their mounts and told them when it was time to leave the barn, venturing in the direction of the training track. Interacting with the stable vet, Dr. Matthews, and being at the feed man's side as the hay, straw, and oats were delivered was part of the daily routine. The blacksmith checked with him about which horses were ready to be shod, asking if any special shoeing was required.

When sets went to the track for clocked workouts, Raymond joined the trainer, who gave him every opportunity to observe and ask questions. Other than to say good morning, he stayed away from getting involved with the jockeys' agents who were in and out of the area on a regular basis. The only one who could make a commitment to them about their jockey riding a certain horse was Joe. When owners came to the barn, if the boss was tied up, he greeted the visitors promptly, showing them their horses and properly referring training and racing schedule questions back to the trainer. The assistant understood the limits of his position. The stable help talked to him freely as he moved around.

Raymond was knowledgeable, personable, and busy controlling the stable's activities as a qualified assistant trainer should be. This young man had finally found the answer to his vocational uncertainty. Right then, he belonged to that rare breed called horsemen.

One racing afternoon, as Joe saddled a fidgety horse for a race, Raymond stood attentively at his side. The trainer struggled, asserting, "Steady, boy. Hold still." Ready to jump in and help, the assistant moved closer to Joe.

"Need help?"

"No. I got him, thanks. This one always tries my patience."

After the saddling, Joe and Raymond walked into the paddock enclosure where the owners were expecting their horses, trainers, and jockeys to arrive. When they reached that area, he suddenly saw the exquisite woman that had previously taken away his breath. Looking eagerly in her direction, he asked Joe, "Who is that beauty?" The old-timer was caught off guard. "Beauty . . . where?" Nodding his head in the proper direction, he said, "The lovely one over there, the lady wearing the peach-colored dress."

"That's Suzanne Brockhurst, the racetrack chairman's daughter. You certainly, have expensive taste." "No, sir . . . Great taste!" The older gentleman could still appreciate young love. "Good luck. She is a stake filly in every sense of the word. That lady has class." Being captivated, Raymond expressed his emotionally beating heart once more with an "I feel the ground shaking."

CHAPTER 7
The Trainer

Standing outside his barn with Raymond, the boss had a tough conversation to undertake. "Son, I'll be gone for a few days or so. Need some routine checkups in the hospital. Haven't been feeling right. Must be getting old." "No, you aren't, but doing what the doctor advises is always worthwhile . . . Don't worry about the stable while you are gone. I'll keep things moving along. Take care of yourself." "The phone won't be far away. You'll be hearing from me. My clients all know of the situation. I'm not the least bit worried." Reassuring Joe, he said, "I won't disappoint you or them. The stable will run the same as if you were here. I'll try hard to win races for you. Everything will move along just fine." Again, expressing his total confidence in Raymond: "No doubt, you will hold the fort. Besides all the owners like you. It should be smooth sailing. I don't see any drawbacks, and I'll be around before you know it." "Get better, that's the only concern."

Several days had passed, and Raymond was sitting at Joe's desk. The phone rang; it was the patient making his first call from the hospital to the barn. "Good morning. Did I catch you at a good time to talk? What is happening?"

"No problems here. How are you? I have been worried."

"The doctors aren't too happy with what they are finding . . . It's time for me to call it quits." The news was stunning.

"Don't want to hear that. Joe, racing is your life."

"No regrets. I lived my own way through all the years. Now listen, I recommended to my clients that you are ready to go out on your own.

46

Brad Phillips, Justin Cox, and Mr. and Mrs. De Leo are willing to give you a chance to train for them. That group will give you fifteen horses in total to start with. Not a bad beginning for a young lad. What do you think of that?" Words were hard to come by.

"Wow, this is unexpected."

"You earned it. Do what I know you can do."

"Yes, sir. My heart is in training. What an opportunity. I'll be forever grateful. Thank you isn't ever going to be enough." At the end of the conversation, Raymond had mixed emotions. This was the chance of a lifetime, but he realized that his friend was ill, perhaps very ill. Consistent with his forward planning, Joe arranged that the other horses previously under his care that were leaving the barn would be sent, in short order, to the different trainers selected by their owners. Then Raymond would be on his own and able to concentrate with the remaining runners.

The racetrack had a new trainer, a dream made possible by diligence, good fortune, self-confidence, and some serious prayers. Josephine said the rosary for her only son every night. Raymond was off to the races! While working as the assistant trainer for Joe Hardy, Raymond had become friendly with other owners. The racetrack was an easy place for insiders to meet other racing people because most of them were outgoing, readily socializing with other horsemen. They were a unique bunch that shared a common bond in that sport regardless of their backgrounds, education, or wealth. In that group was Bruno La Scala. When that horse owner heard that Raymond, whom he had met, was on his own, Bruno immediately spoke with the new trainer.

They agreed that two of his horses would be quickly sent to Raymond's barn. The new trainer felt a sense of excitement; another owner had taken note of his achievement and sought him out. It was a clear, breezy Saturday afternoon, only two weeks after the Bruno horses had arrived that Raymond had one of them, Tenor, running in the third race.

On that race day, the crowds were pouring through the turnstiles into the racetrack. Some track personnel at nearby entrance stands were peddling tout sheets while others were hawking programs and pencils. Cars were lined up outside on the boulevard, waiting to gain entry. Horns were being blown by a few impatient gamblers. At a stable security gate, a quarter mile off the public entrance, a metallic-blue 1965 Mustang convertible, white top-down, passed through.

The driver, Raymond, clean-cut as usual, wearing a blue blazer, gray pants, gray shirt, a blue-and-light-gray stripped tie, and black shoes, waved to the uniformed security guard. The green-and-gold sticker on his windshield read, "Trainer." The young man took pride in that status emblem, and the way he dressed reflected that sentiment. It was early afternoon as he began this drive to his stable. At that time of day, the stable area was extremely quiet and peaceful compared to the hustle and bustle of the morning training hours when hundreds of racehorses were going back and forth to be trained. These equine athletes were now resting in their stalls while many of the grooms, who cared for them and were up at 5:00 a.m., now indulged in taking a nap.

Continuing to drive until he reached barn number 10, Raymond noticed a new Mercedes-Benz sitting at the far end of his barn. The 6-feet-plus, 185 lb. trainer parked then briskly walked past an engraved oak sign placed above the sliding barn door that read, "Raymond Masterson, Trainer." It always commanded a proud glance from him as he walked past.

There he found two men inside the barn, one of whom he recognized as Bruno, the owner of the horse racing that day. His client, 5 feet, 10 inches, mid-forties, wore a high-quality tailored dark brown sport jacket, tan slacks, opened white shirt, and brown designer shoes. His hair was styled, fingernails manicured, and his overall physical appearance would imply that he went to the gym several times a week. He might easily fall into the category of a dapper Dan.

The younger man, about Raymond's age, slightly shorter than the owner, was unshaven and built like a wrestler, thereby giving a rough and ready appearance even though, he wore a black sports jacket and denim jeans. This dude didn't go to the gym. He was the gym!

A greeting smile was offered. "Hey, Bruno, what brings you here so early? Making sure your horse looks good?" The owner was annoyed by the interrogation, or, more appropriately, by the interruption, "Hell no, Ray. Sonny and I are here making sure that Tenor wins!" Quickly, the trainer observed that the other man had a syringe in his large right hand.

Glancing into the stall, he saw blood on the neck of Bruno's horse. Raymond looked at the imposing man with the needle. "What's going on here? Are you drugging my horse?" A sharp answer came from the tough guy: "Yeah, you gotta problem? Whatta do you think, you own it?" Judging that the trainer was becoming noticeably uncomfortable, Bruno became concerned, for this was not a favorable trait under these circumstances. Raymond had not been expected to be there, and these two believed that they were on a hit-and-disappear mission! Trying to calm him down, Bruno said, "Look, Ray boy, relax. After the races today, you'll have a ton of money in your pocket. I'm gonna make you rich. Go ahead, Sonny, tell him."

A diplomat he was not. Sonny went for the bottom line. "Play your cards right. Take the money or else." The dismayed trainer repeatedly shook his head. "I'm not looking for that kind of money. Drugging horses isn't how I win. It's dead wrong. I don't want any part of this!" Trying to get Raymond to see it his way, using a big brother approach, the boss softened up. "Ray, listen to me. You can't make money on anything honest. Learn that. Don't screw this up for Sonny, for me, for you, for the boys! Today is a day to pick up pocket cash. Come on. We are all in this together."

This talk was smooth, but Raymond wasn't buying it. He was raised differently. "You are pushing me off a cliff. Why didn't you ask first?" Since this line of underworld logic wasn't working, Bruno put aside his effort to reason with Raymond and got tough. "I don't want to hear any more bullshit! Your approval wasn't needed. These are my horses . . . no? Who pays the fucking bills every month? Now, I'm going over to the clubhouse, but Sonny will stay at your side, and you can both walk over with the horse together, real close together. He will be watching your every move, so no mistakes because you're gonna get hurt, or maybe the rest of your horses are gonna get hurt!"

Sonny's curt, self- serving smile expressed a wish that a mistake would take place. Tenor's groom arrived, preparing his horse with a good brushing, last-minute touches, then placing the racing bridle on him. Finally, the call came over the loudspeaker in the barn, "Bring your horse to the paddock for the third race." The Thoroughbred, along with his groom and a hot walker, departed the barn with Raymond and Sonny close behind them. No words were exchanged during the ten-minute walk, but the trainer was desperately trying to figure some way out.

As they reached the entry path to the paddock, two- armed security guards stood on each side of the entrance and greeted Raymond. Was this an answer? Could they save the day? Although he had not seen a weapon, he had every reason to believe that Sonny carried one. A cry for help now might only make matters dramatically worse; if not now, certainly later!

His better judgment forced him not to view this as a way out. After the horse was saddled, Raymond found a place in the lower corner area of the clubhouse to watch the race alone. "Tenor" won easily, paying fifteen dollars for two, but there was no joy for the trainer, who did not even participate in the winner's circle photograph. Dejectedly, he walked back to the barn to await the horse's return. As he sat in his office, Bruno and his buddy eventually arrived, both on a high.

Reaching into his pocket, Bruno took out a wad of bills, which he threw onto the desk. "Here's two thousand cash. See how fucking easy it was, and all you did was complain!" This gesture brought no delight to the distraught trainer.

"I don't want it!"

"How can anybody be that stupid?"

"You keep it!" was Raymond's firm response.

"Okay, stupido, work for nothing if it makes you happy, but as far as I'm concerned, you knew that the horse was drugged before it ran, and you grabbed the two thousand. Get the picture? Talk about what happened today, and you're in deep shit. Fucker, I own you!" The road ahead that this trainer saw was dark and long. Some signs flashed, "Dangerous curve ahead. Slow down," and the last weather-beaten sign read, "Dead End." This was a dim glimpse of his future with Bruno in the picture!

The only thread of hope was that Bruno might remove the horses from his barn and send them to another trainer. The incident with the drugging of "Tenor" would slowly fade away, and life would again become normal. However, every day for the following three weeks, Bruno called or stopped at the barn to check on his horses. When he decided that it was time for them to run, Raymond was ordered to place them in two different races on the same day's racing card. When the overnight racing schedule for the following day was posted, "Tenor" would run in the eighth race and "A Shortcut" in the ninth.

By chance, this was a gambler's dream. The betting prospects with this setup were numerous. There was a late daily double, exacters, and triples in each race along with the standard win, place, and show bets. If anyone could hit all those bets, they would need an armored car to take the money home.

On that race day, he chose not to perform the normal ritual of going home to eat, shower, and change his clothes. Raymond stayed at the barn. Perhaps he might stop the inevitable, but that was beyond a long shot. As he feared, it was about 2:00 p.m. when the gangsters showed up. Meeting them head-on in the shed row, he asked the obvious question, "Are you going to drug both of them?" A sharp answer came from Sonny, "Yeah. Two is always better than one except in broken legs."

These other words easily slipped out of the boss's mouth. "We have been through this garbage once before. Don't waste my time." It was impossible for the trainer not to plead his case, but they were deaf to him. Meanwhile, his attempt for salvation was aggravating the visitors. It was the time for the muscle to play his part, sliding his right hand under his chin, then moving it away at a 45-degree angle, an Italian gesture that one uses when they perceived a conversation as total nonsense, going nowhere. Sonny glared, placed his unshaven face in front of Raymond's face, and in a flash, he roughly pushed the trainer aside, who automatically, without thinking, shoved back. Not a smart move to make.

It triggered the enforcer to revert to his gangland etiquette. The horseman received a punishing right-handed blow to the ribs, which was rapidly followed by an equally hard punch to the stomach. The stunned trainer doubled over, falling quickly to the ground. It was time to put the finishing touch to the beating with some well-placed kicks. As Sonny's powerful leg started to move forward, the trainer rolled over, grabbing a pitchfork leaning against a wall.

Raymond lashed out, solidly jabbing the bottom of the kicker's right black shoe. The surprised attacker jerked backward, lost his footing, momentarily stumbling before regaining balance. The second that he stood firmly on his feet Sonny reached effortlessly inside his jacket pocket from where a pistol handle appeared. Having been physically passive to this point and contented to watch the beating, the boss was forced to boldly thrust a right hand against his underling's strong arm, giving an order, "Sonny, stop. Put it away! This ain't the place or the time to kill him."

Visibly, the bully restrained himself by clenching his fists. The owner then glared directly at Raymond, giving a definitive ultimatum, "Enough! I've had it. These horses run OR ELSE! Understand?" Using the wall for support to get up, then to stand up, Raymond was finally erect, trying to catch his breath. Shaking off the pain, the young man was yet too dazed to respond, but would not have known what to utter even if he had the ability. What do you say to gangsters with guns when they want it their way or no way?

Still considering the trainer as prey, Sonny was weighing his options; however, Bruno expressed other concerns to the trainer. "You know what I want. No ifs or buts. Nothing could be simpler . . . They run. I'm done here!" Viciously both gangsters looked back as they left with Bruno putting his hand under the arm of his slightly limping partner. There was a large, wooden supply box located between two stalls on which Raymond sat. Dropping his head in deep thought, he wondered, "God, what did I get myself into?"

After a period of deliberation, he finally decided on a course of action. The trainer nodded several times with lukewarm conviction, got up, brushed himself off, walking to his top-down Mustang convertible. Driving around the stable area between barns and across freshly harrowed horse paths, Raymond passed several veterinarians' vehicles that he recognized but didn't stop until he found the one that was sought, pulling alongside it.

Waiting in his car, Raymond looked for his vet, Dr. Matthews, a burly, tall man in his early forties, a former football star offensive end at Ohio State. As he arrived, the trainer gingerly got out of the car, and slowly started the conversation, "Dr. Matthews, I'm in a lot of trouble." The vet could not help but give the trainer an obvious once-over. This was not the same clean-cut, cheerful person that he spoke with every morning.

"I would say so. Looks like you ran into a train. What's up?" "Feel worse than I look, and the train has a name, but that's not my problem right now. Doc, do you trust me?" What the trainer needed was complete, unquestioned confidence for his request so that he would be able to continue the tale.

The answer came back without a hitch, "Of course. No reason why not to. Tell me what's going on the best you can, then I will see where we are at?", So, the story began to unfold as far as it could be told. "I have two horses running today. They must be scratched, taken out of their races" "Hum, not an easy order to fill, especially on a busy Saturday. Lots of bettors. The stewards will throw a fit. What do you have in mind?" "Only a vet can do this. If you report that the horses had colic and you treated them, then the stewards have no comeback. Medicated horses can't run." There was a hesitated, calculating moment. "Risky, but it sounds possible. Will there be anybody else at the barn?"

"Only us, I promise."

"Okay. If you need it, let's get to work." With Doc in pursuit, Raymond drove directly to his barn. When they arrived, the vet slid open the left-side panel of the truck, withdrew two vials of colic medicine, needles, and syringes. Rolling up his sleeves, he followed the trainer to a stall and when they entered. Raymond held that horse by its halter with the bronze name plate, "Tenor." The vet found a trace of blood on the neck of Bruno's horse. This observation went without comment but not without concern, "Who is next?"

Led to another horse, the bronze name plate on this halter read, "A Shortcut." Again, the vet became aware of discoloration on the horse's neck, but this time, rubbed over the spot with his thumb. He remained silent as he treated the animal but was quickly drawing his own obvious conclusions as to what happened. "We are all done here. You got what was needed. What are their names?"

"A Shortcut" and "Tenor" both belong to La Scala Stable." Scribbling the information on a pad, he slipped it back into his side pocket. "Raymond, believe me, I would not have done this for anyone else. This is way out there. Be careful!" The warning was acknowledged. "I sure will try."

Giving his veterinarian friend complete, undivided attention, the trainer prayed for some needed insight. Dr. Matthews sensed that the trainer was seeking help for a solution, but he had little to offer. The best that he could say was, "I do not like what we did and what is happening here spells some serious trouble. There is not much that I can tell you. These aren't good people that you are dealing with, which is an understatement."

"No question. This is unbelievable, but I'll have to figure it out by myself. For now, there aren't any easy answers." "You're right, but one thing is for certain, you can always count on me." There was one last piece of serious advice rendered, "Maybe you should get the hell out of here. Go somewhere else. This place isn't safe." The decision had already been made. "There is no place to hide.

Maybe I can talk my way out." When the doctor departed, he gave the trainer a strong long-lasting handshake with a departing, "Good luck." Standing straight but alone, Raymond stared down at a long, empty shed row as the vet disappeared. It was the quiet before the storm!

CHAPTER 8
The Scratch

*I*t was time for him to enter his combined tack room and office. In the back right-hand corner were three wooden horses with a polished leather saddle sitting on each. Blinkers and bridles hung in rows from bronze hook sets arranged on a board affixed to a panel. A large doorless metal cabinet, flush against a wall, was filled with liniments, salves, bandages, and other items used daily as needed in any racing stable. Diagonally placed at the opposite side of the room, across from the saddles, was a modern desk that hosted a lamp, a phone, and a mix of condition books used to find races in which the horses could be entered to run. Some racing magazines were scattered alongside them and were read to keep up with current industry trends and stories related to the racing world. A hardwood plank floor was swept clean. The office, although uncomplicated, displayed good taste, organization, and masculinity.

Experiencing a surge of courage, Raymond grabbed the phone before drawing a final deep breath regarding his decision. It was time for the stewards to be drawn into the picture. Right or wrong, he would place into action the move that had been carefully planned. It had to be done soon. There wasn't any time to procrastinate! The answer to success or failure would soon follow; he could not predict the future!

"The stewards, please. Hello, Mr. Ridgley. This is Raymond Masterson. You know I have two horses running today, "Tenor" and "A Short Cut" in the eighth and ninth races. They both came down with colic and were treated by my vet, Dr. Matthews. I want both to be scratched."

At that moment, Raymond heard an unusual noise in the shed row. He believed the worst; the gangsters had returned? There was no other choice but to check the disturbance, putting the steward on hold.

"Excuse me a second . . ."

Cautiously, Raymond walked out of the office door, hoping that the bad guys had not arrived. If those people entered his office at that precise moment, it would be an explosive situation. They'd probably rip the phone from its connection and some part of his body immediately thereafter. In his relief, he found that a broom had fallen off from a half-broken wall bracket, causing it to land noisily in the shed row. Regaining his composure, he returned inside the office, closed the door, and promptly spoke again with the steward. "I'm back. Sir, are they scratched? . . . Thank you."

The stewards required documentation from the veterinarian to back up the reason for the animals to be taken off the race card. Acknowledging the demand, he promptly concurred. "I will have Dr. Matthew's report at your office first thing in the morning." Steward Ridgley, who had received the call, offered his personal regrets, "Tough break, but there will be other days." "Yes, sir . . . Very bad luck." Hanging up, he waited to bear the wrath of Bruno and Sonny after they heard that the two horses were not running!

On a Saturday, most boxes in the clubhouse were filled. Richly and properly dressed patrons moved around, socializing, discussing that day's race. There was never a loss for stories at the racetrack. The avid gossiper may possibly not even bet on a race, for it would take up too much talk time. At the track, any of that day's program changes were announced over the loudspeaker. Announcer: "We have two late scratches, "Tenor" in the eighth and "A Shortcut" in the ninth. All advanced wagering on these horses will be refunded. The rest of the card remains unchanged at this time." Staring at each other in disbelief, the gangsters' mouths were wide open, but they were speechless. Their blood pressure readings skyrocketed off the chart. Slamming his racing paper to the ground,

Sonny leaned aggressively over to Bruno. He couldn't wait to get the first words out of his slimy mouth, "I'm gonna kill him. Don't try to stop me!" Bruno wasn't interested in hearing Sonny's irrational solution to the problem even if only he was irrational for the moment. He had an overpowering, compulsive thought and command, "Back to the barn!" The soldier was uncertain. Should Bruno be present? This was going to be an ugly confrontation. "Maybe you shouldn't be there, boss? I can handle it!"

There was nothing to talk about it. "Shut up. Back to the barn now! I want to see this prick bleed!" As he waited for the confrontation, the target tapped his fingers in an irregular beat on the desktop, muttering to himself, "How could this happen? It all started out so right. Everything has been incredible." The trainer started to vividly recollect the events that got him there. His mind wandered, but in a flash, it soon came back to earth. A car door slammed shut, then another. The expected visitors had arrived.

Raymond believed that these could be his last minutes before eternity, the thought of imminent death was not easily dismissed. Boldly entering the barn, they immediately passed the groom, Andre, who was raking the shed row. Andre had returned from Mexico, going to work for Raymond. Always showing respect to the owners, he unknowingly greeted these two intruders in a friendly manner, "Buenos tardes."

They walked past him as though he was a pole or didn't exist. Andre kept raking. It was not his to question why. In short order, another person walked through the same opened sliding front door of the barn, then moved along the same path as the gangsters. He rolled up his sleeves to be comfortable as he always did before starting work. Ahead, Raymond's office door was closed but unlocked. Sonny turned the knob shoving it open; both hoodlums rushed in! In a second, words forcefully shot out of Bruno's mouth,

"You did it! You fucked us! You son of a bitch!"

Stopping after several steps, Bruno backed up, blocking any possible escape through that entrance. Raymond wasn't looking to run away, but deep in his mind, he truly hoped for a miracle. He zealously stated his only defense, "I couldn't do what you wanted. This isn't my thing! "Tenor's" win still has me sick!"

The words were wasted. The gangsters sought no excuses; they had no intention to talk! Sonny zeroed in on his target, throwing him against the metal storage cabinet. Items flew, some glass containers broke, liquids spread as they rolled around the floor! The trainer tried to defend himself and quickly realized that he must bring Sonny down onto the ground to give himself any chance of long-term survival! Wrapping his arms around Sonny in a bear hug, he boldly jumped on the same right foot that had been previously stabbed with the pitchfork. The attacker flinched, giving Raymond the momentary edge to wrestle him down.

As they rolled, Sonny's pistol, a compact .40 caliber Beretta, slid loose. Keeping his back near to the opened door, Bruno watched intensely, expecting to see plenty of blood. Suddenly, he felt a hand on his shoulder spinning him around. There stood Dr. Matthews, who promptly landed a solid right on Bruno's jaw, bringing the mobster down for the count of eight, nine, ten, out! The vet then advanced to concentrate on Sonny, who was all over Raymond, ready to deliver crushing blows! He grabbed Sonny by the back of his long hair. The tough guy immediately shot up from the ground to an upright position. They exchanged blows, each one expressing facial pains as they were hit.

Finally, the vet realized that it was time to deliver a perfectly placed knee to Sonny's groin. Thud, Done! As Sonny started to bend over in agony, the vet clasped his strong two hands together, slamming them down on the back of Sonny's neck, lowering the gangster head, introducing it to his knee. At that moment, there was a sharp crack, Sonny's face became bright red. The mobster stumbled sideways, uncontrollably bumping against the desk, which moved two feet sideways on impact. His left hand went to his groin while the right one feebly searched for his pistol, which was no longer there. The hood was still standing but barely, if he had ever taken a beating, this day was the day!

At hearing the constant ruckus, Andre suddenly entered the action. Seeing Bruno trying to get up, he placed his dirty, manure-stained boot over the boss's right shoulder, holding him on the floor. On the other side of the room, Sonny continued to sadly struggle to set his body upright. Not taking any chances, Raymond kicked the Beretta to the corner of the office while directing Andre regarding Bruno, "Let him up but watch him."

The groom removed his foot, and Bruno awkwardly started to stand after several, half-assed, failed efforts. Andre was prepared to send him back to the floor if he showed any fight. Raymond, in his better judgment, checked Bruno for another weapon but did not find one. Dr. Matthews, who was bloodied and noticeably out of breath, forced himself to stand tall, ready to inflict more damage if it might be necessary. Looking at Bruno then Sonny, Raymond then showed no hint of fear in his voice. He was all business, "I want you useless, no accounts out of here! Get out . . . Now!"

Slowly, the intruders painfully staggered to the exit. Bruno didn't turn back but threatened, "You will pay for this! You just entered hell!" At the door, Sonny, in defiance, erratically spit a mouthful of blood onto the wooden floor. Together with Bruno he moved back down the shed row although much differently from how they arrived. The swagger was gone.

Dr. Matthews was worthy to be in the spotlight. "Doc, you picked the right time to show up." "I was worried about you." He stopped talking to catch his wind, which required several deep breaths. "When I saw a car outside that I didn't recognize, I figured you could use some backup." Being obviously grateful, Raymond was still a bit curious. "Great call. You saved my life! Where did you learn the moves and how to street fight?"

Reluctantly revealing a little of his past, he said, "Well, everybody knows I played football in college, which is a get-knocked-down game and get- back- up. It toughens the body and willpower. The thought of quitting doesn't exist. It is important to show everybody that you can take it. "What I never mentioned to anyone before, and let's keep it between us, that when young and foolish in high school, I rode bulls for three years but finally had to quit. The broken bones were starting to add up, and the bulls were getting smarter, and I wasn't. A bad combination, but that is where the quick moves developed.

On a bull's back, things happened in fast time. You move before you think. It is all instinct. As far as fights went at the rodeo or after a tough, grudge football game, I never walked away from a brawl. Sometimes, but not too often, I was so beaten up that I couldn't walk away. Sober memories have come back.

Today was not my first battle. I feel eighteen again!" The vet offered a conclusion regarding the outcome, "This fight was over with two lucky knee shots. That crumb never expected them." A quick joke was offered by the trainer, "Maybe he should have ridden bulls." The gun on the floor presented a problem. The vet asked, "Do you want it?" The trainer shook his head side to side. "No thanks. I have a 20-gauge shotgun. That's plenty for any hunting coming my way."

Dr. Matthews stated, "We can't let it sit there or take it to a police station. They would ask too many questions, which you can't answer, and I don't want to be involved. Let me take it and add the toy to my collection . . . The story behind this one is priceless." Doc picked the pistol up from the ground, placing the weapon in his pocket. They firmly shook hands. It was time for Dr. Matthews to patch and clean himself, returning to the image of a respected veterinarian.

The final step in closing the event was to give a word of caution to Andre. The trainer placed a hand on his friend's shoulder and asked for secrecy, "You saw nothing." The groom nodded his head in an affirmative way. "Entiendo." With time to think, Raymond was trying desperately to find some way to solve this unbelievable problem. Being vulnerable, he dwelt on seeking an answer, and the answer always came up the same, call Uncle Vito. If not him, who?"

He remembered what his mother had continually told him, "Don't get involved in anything with my brother." As the years went by, he fully understood why she was worried and why obeying her was the right thing to do, but this wasn't business. This was a real life-and-death situation, his life or death! If desperation needed an example, this was it! Stay-away time was over! Self-preservation dictated that he make the call. The trainer dialed his uncle's home and was greeted him with the customary, "Hello, hello." But it wasn't Vito on the line.

"Hi, Aunt Irene, this is Raymond."

"How are you?"

"I'm fine, and yourself?"

"An ache here or there, otherwise fine. What's going on with you?"

"I would like to visit Uncle Vito tonight if it is possible?"

"Of course, I know he will be home all this evening. He's not going to the restaurant or anywhere else. What time are you thinking?"

"How about . . . around eight?"

"Come over earlier. Eat with us. That would be nice. We don't see you enough."

"It would be hard to get there any sooner. I'm still at the barn and need to clean up a bit but thank you." The conversation concluded by repeating the arrival time and a warm goodbye. Her love and concern were authentic, to be appreciated.

Upon arriving at Vito's well-maintained two-story home located on Colonial Road, an exclusive, wealthy Bay Ridge section of Brooklyn, the nephew parked his car in the double wide driveway. All the houses on this street had well-manicured lawns and shrubs worthy of beautifying an area that overlooked the Narrows. This special body of water, the entry to New York's Harbor, was spanned by the newly opened Verrazano-Narrows bridge. The longest suspension bridge in the Western Hemisphere. It comfortably connected the New York boroughs of Staten Island and Brooklyn. Driving time over this span was a far faster ride than the twenty-five minutes, five and- a-half-mile sea trip offered by the old Staten Island Ferry.

The nostalgic ferry ride, established in 1817, was still available with no charge for the voyage. Here was a rare chance to relax and go back to the past for free. Raymond observed the view and recalled that the family took the Staten Island Ferry when going from Brooklyn to Vineland, New Jersey, by way of the New Jersey Turnpike. They left the pike at the Bordentown exit with another sixty-two miles to travel before reaching the family farmhouse. Arriving at the door, Aunt Irene greeted him with a welcome hug and two kisses. "Come in, dear. You look a little tired. Are you tired?"

"This has been a tough day, but I'm getting my strength back."

"So glad to hear that you are feeling better . . ."

The aunt was not quite convinced about her nephew's state of mind or body. She knew Raymond well, and he didn't seem to be completely himself. "Are you sure you are alright? Nothing is wrong is there?" She was a woman with a sixth sense regarding these matters.

"No, everything is fine. I just need to go over something with Uncle Vito. It's not—it's not important."

"Your uncle is waiting for you. He's in the TV room and has been anxious for you to get here."

When Raymond entered the TV room, Vito stood up to greet and embrace him. His uncle gestured with an inviting hand for them to sit down. The nephew started the session "I'm so glad that you were free tonight. Did you hear what happened to me?" A serious expression came over Vito's face. He dropped his chin, nodding strongly while giving an ice-cold stare. "Yeah, I hear everything. Too late on this one. I shoulda known earlier that you were involved with this La Scala creep. I would -of ended it fast."

Lowering his head, Raymond was almost ashamed to continue after hearing his uncle speak. "I'm confused and worried . . . don't know what to do. I'm embarrassed to bring this mess to you."

"You are dealing with scum. Bruno is lower than a snake. Let me hear your side of the story."

"This afternoon, I caught Bruno and Sonny drugging their horses again. Sonny gave a shot to "Tenor" three weeks ago, and Bruno forced me to run him. The horse won easily, and after the race, I was offered two thousand, but I refused to take it. Bruno said that it didn't matter. I was involved, that he owned me."

"Over my dead body. That idiot will never own a Di Mario," growled Vito. "So, you got smart, got tough?"

"I hope so, not too sure. I scratched the drugged horses that were supposed to run today."

"That took balls. Then what happened?"

"As soon as the two found out, they came back to work me over. I felt like a dead man! Sonny was ready to punch away, when, luckily, my vet showed up. He beat the hell out of them! You should have seen it!"

"He should- of killed them! Why did he stop?" asked Vito. "Anyway, their story has a different twist. They claimed that you and the vet jumped them from behind with clubs as they came to . . . talk.

"That is a damn lie!"

"I figured that much. It didn't take any imagination. They are sneaky bastards. You can't find out the right day of the week from them, but regardless, you are in a tough spot . . . I have a meeting tomorrow night with someone who can help . . . Let's hope for the best!"

"I'm expecting Bruno won't leave me alone. Those bums, were wild, making all kinds of threats!"

"Nobody is going to physically hurt you without facing me! They're gonna know my position. After that, I'm not damn sure . . . what goes down. I don't control them. It could get ugly very fast. Even I might not be able to stop other things from happening!"

"I'm giving you a lot of trouble. It's the last thing you need. Should I leave?"

"I don't wanna hear that. Forget it! That's what uncles are for--- period!"

The Mafia boss didn't want to chase the subject matter any further; it had been exhausted. "Hey, there is a good game on tonight, the Giants are playing the Dodgers. One of these teams will win the pennant. Relax, stay and watch it with me." Grabbing the remote, Vito turned on the TV. The two men sat back, crossed their legs, sharing the ball game together. It became a family night.

Uncle Vito's meeting with Tommy Z was already initiated even before Raymond had told his story or made a request for help. That was the way the Godfather operated—behind the scenes, ahead of the game. It is what kept him on top and alive!

CHAPTER 9
Romance Is in the Air

Early the next morning, Raymond stood by the outside rail of the track, watching his horses train. Spotting Suzanne not too far away, he decided to walk over toward that location. What was there to lose? The trainer was starting at ground zero. As the lady stood in an open grassy area, she was aware of his approaching.

Reaching her, Romeo concentrated on maintaining a casual composure and a clear tone in his voice. "Good morning. You are the best-dressed lady on the grounds." There was a chance on simple, old fashioned flattery working. The lady was openly friendly.

"Thank you for the compliment . . . I am Suzanne Brockhurst, and I'm certain that I have seen you at the races."

"A pleasure to meet you. I'm Raymond Masterson. No doubt we have passed each other in the afternoon. May I join you?"

"Of course, Masterson . . . Masterson. Aren't you the trainer who had to scratch several horses yesterday?"

"Yes, that was me."

"If I may ask, what happened?"

"Not a secret. They needed to be treated for colic." The lady was surprised. "Two in one day and on race day, most unusual."

"Yes, unfortunately."

A conclusion from her was forthcoming. "That will probably never happen again." It was impossible to agree more affirmatively. "Not if I can help it!" He never felt stronger about predicting any future event.

At the same time, their eyes automatically scanned back to the track, watching their horses; there was a lull in talking.

In his mind, it was important for him not to be overly anxious or uninteresting, so he continued paying attention to the horses in training, but finally, the trainer felt the necessity to continue the dialogue anyway possible. Turning sideways to have her in his complete field of vision, he asked a question, "Where are your horses?" Waving her hand, she pointed past the finish line. "Right there."

"Still galloping strongly," was Raymond's observation.

"That is our trainer's way."

"He knows what he is doing. Mr. Weatherbe is an accomplished horseman," volunteered the young trainer.

"It has been fifteen years that he has trained for our family. We would be lost without him." In the distance, the Brockhurst horses have finished their gallop and were pulled up, ready to leave the track.

"Oh well. It is time for returning to the barn . . . Glad you took the time to visit." The young trainer again faced her directly and closed with a sincere, "Hope there will be other mornings to say hello." The earlier part of the day turned out to be pleasant, but there was still the remainder to be completed.

Saddling a horse for the sixth race that afternoon, Raymond was aware of the usual crowd of people watching the procedure, a customary ritual for some bettors. Before placing their good money down, it was important for some of them to see the racehorse. They wanted to observe if the animal was nervous. Did the horse's coat have a shine? Was it carrying the proper weight with obvious muscle tone of a fit Thoroughbred? Ultimately, did the horse look like a winner to them?

Raymond casually scanned the crowd, looking for a friendly face, someone he knew to whom he might wave or smile at. This day was no exception, he followed his normal routine. It was not a good day for that gesture! There, within thirty feet, standing motionless, a bruised but arrogant Sonny glared hatefully at him. He did not blink or move a facial muscle or, as a matter of fact, any part of his body. It was the equivalent of looking at a damaged rock statue. The gangster just continued to stare! If looks could kill, Raymond was a dead man!

Naturally, the trainer became unsettled, slowly turning away while trying not to show the least stress from intimidation. This was a predicament that did not have any precedent during his life. There was no way to expect or prepare for this type of confrontation. Taking the only way out available, he forced himself to concentrate on saddling by paying complete attention to the task at hand. All his movements were slow and deliberate, rechecking the girth strap and blinkers several times. He wanted no spare time to gaze or think. When the Thoroughbred had been saddled, it was necessary for him to leave that area for the box area. Raymond found himself compelled, although unwise, to scan the crowd again. He was ready to return Sonny's stare, which would have solved nothing.

Luckily, Sonny was gone, but the message clearly remained! Several days later, during morning training hours, Suzanne, standing by the racetrack rail, was holding an opened umbrella, staying dry from the light rain. The trainer, wearing a black raincoat over his clothes, joined her. She quickly offered to share the covering, so being the taller, Raymond reached for it. He took the umbrella and held it slightly inclined to be certain that the lady got the major share of protection. It was an opportunity to show that he was a considerate gentleman.

With stopwatch in hand, it was time to clock the workouts of her family's horses. She moved it up and down in her hand. "I never get the time quite right. It is a lost art." Firmly the start/stop button was pressed. After the horses passed the finish line, she again slid her thumb against that button. "Let me see. A half mile in forty-eight seconds."

"Decent move on this track, and they seemed to be doing it without much effort," was his response. Attempting to place the stopwatch back into her purse, it dropped, causing the expensive object to fall onto the wet ground. Raymond reacted quickly, bending over. "I got it." The lady apologized. "How clumsy of me, Sorry." Not wanting her to feel embarrassed, these words were promptly said, "I drop mine all the time. For some reason, they are slippery." The stopwatch was picked up and rubbed with a clean handkerchief taken out from a pocket. Once dried, he slowly placed it in her hand with a gentle motion that glided his fingers over the skin of her soft hand. The starstruck lover had touched her! They looked at each other.

There was a definite moment of electricity, but in a courteous manner, she quickly showed her composure by thanking him, "How thoughtful." Under what seemed to be friendly circumstances, Raymond decided to take a chance and ask for a date. "Could we possibly get together for a dinner? Any night would be okay."

"Oh, I am afraid not. . . You see, I've been going out with—" Instinctively, the listener interrupted, he didn't want to hear too much and become discouraged or forgo any chance that the future might hold. "Please, no need to explain. Perhaps some other time." Not desiring to hurt Raymond's feelings, she was relieved that her polite rejection was cut short, then in a positive manner. She responded, "Yes, perhaps another time." Again, they parted ways.

A week had passed when, once more, Raymond saw Suzanne standing by the rail, a short distance away, watching her family's horses train. A tall, extremely well-built fellow in a short-sleeve sport shirt, dungarees, and cowboy boots was at her side. They were in deep, attentive conversation. Rationalizing, this guy was more than likely the reason she did not accept a dinner date with him. Raymond was naturally taken aback. From that distance, his competition looked formidable, but occasionally, time changes things, and he had plenty of time. At a point, Suzanne caught sight of him and gave a friendly wave.

He likewise returned the acknowledgment but was certain that to walk over and speak or interrupt them would have been foolhardy. Besides, he didn't really want to meet the guy in her life, at least not then. Again. he thought that time, perhaps a lot of time would change the landscape to his advantage. He also could not escape a humbling thought: what did he materially have to offer this lady in comparison to her wealth, a cabin for a castle?' Only Cupid, who had let the arrow fly, knew of the complexity of his male target. The archer realized that the strength of Raymond's deep affection for Suzanne came from a true, loving heart longing for a soul mate! The chasing game was on.

The cherubic little angel had used a generous amount of love potion on that arrowhead, but would it be enough to get Raymond to walk into the sunlight of ecstasy with Suzanne? There would be many obstacles. Somewhere along the road to romance, Cupid would need another arrow especially designed to equally inspire the lady. Love needs two at the same place, at the same time, and touched by mutual passion.

CHAPTER 10
Jockeys

At 9:00 p.m., inside jockey Juan's ranch-style home located at Bethpage, Long Island, other jockeys, their girlfriends, and guests, twenty in all; were partying. Marijuana. coke, along with designer drugs and alcohol were all visible throughout the room. Take one's choice, enjoy, no questions asked. The loud reggae music and drugs had everyone in a festive mood. If you weren't happy, you were dead!

Jockey Juan's girlfriend, Alicia was high. She was all over him: "Juan, you give great parties. I looove them. Si." "Gracias…. And they are only for beautiful women like you." The girlfriend was flattered. She continually slurred her words, as she said, "Youuu, Carlos and Jose, win so, so, so maaany races. You are . . . you are . . . always the top jocks." "We make sure it works that way." Winking at her caused his girlfriend to giggle. He slapped Carlos, standing nearby, on the back then his girlfriend on the back side. A question was thrown from Juan to Carlos, "Carlos, do you ever regret coming to the US?" The answer came spontaneously, "Are you kidding? Where better than this? Lots of money and lots of women who love it."

Juan brought Jose, also in that group, who seemed distant, into the conversation, "Jose, why you so quiet? What's going through your head?" Explaining his pensiveness, he said, "Thinking, wondering where; some of these whacked-out people gonna sleep tonight. They ain't all making it home." Juan had a smart answer, "They sleep where they fall." Everybody laughed, raising their glasses in unison to salute the future fallen.

The doorbell rang, and Juan ordered his companion, "Carlos, go see who that is." That rider became playfully resentful, "Why? You making me the doorman? It's your house." "Because you are so handsome. No pretty woman will scare away." Eating up that answer, Carlos said, "Who can argue that? I'm a lady killer."

Opening the door, he found out, to his disappointment, it wasn't a lady. As big as life, there stood Sonny. "Come on in, the party just started." The Latino did a quick little dance step to prove his point; however, Sonny seemed a bit preoccupied and not interested in the invitation. "It looks great, but I don't have much time. Besides, I already got laid today."

The main interest of this tough guy was getting business done then being on his way. Signaling to Jose and Juan, Carlos pointed to the back bedroom. As they gathered, Sonny, lit a cigarette, then lifted out three large brown envelopes from inside his unzipped black motorcycle jacket and handed each jockey one. Carlos put a hand inside the package, pulling out a fistful of one-hundred-dollar bills and some small bags packed with white powder. The envelope still bulged. The carrier gave them credit. "You jocks are doing a great job." The compliment was returned by Jose, "Amigo, like to see you every day. You are Santa Claus, bringing us gifts all the time."

"You think right. Sonny is your best friend, and there is always room for more cash. Are you guys the best?" Looking to the riders for confirmation, the three nodded yes. The confirmation was verbally expressed by Carlos; "Of course, we the best, and the other jocks we slipped in to work with us are just as good. We take care of them . . . There are no screwups, everybody is happy"

The meeting was closed out by words of future triumphs from Sonny, "We are gonna fuck those bettors to death. We are the team. There ain't no limit." Immediately after the payoff, the bagman departed; he had other gangland chores to perform. Returning to the party, the jockeys hadn't missed a beat during their short absence. Everybody was happy, flying high, with three of the ladies naked.

Meanwhile, Sonny drove directly back to Brooklyn, a forty-minute ride on the Belt Parkway, to the private parking lot behind a clam bar located on Flatbush Avenue and King's Highway. There was no effort required for him to spot the car that he was looking to find; this wasn't the first time. The gangster pulled up alongside a white Caddy, waiting for the occupant to come and enter into his car through the passenger-side door.

Sonny's greeting was to the point, "Richie, you got the green?" "Yeah, of course. Do you think that my pockets are empty? I need the stuff to make another killing." "When are you gonna use it?" "On Friday. I've been running this classy old horse, sore in the last three starts. You couldn't find the sucker in those races finishing up the track, but this designer shit will make him feel like he has new legs and a young heart. It will be a sure win at a good price." The buyer moved his right arm up and down as though pulling the handle on a slot machine, "Cha-ching, cha-ching . . . jackpot!"

The drug dealer automatically agreed. "Yeah . . . Gimme the thousand bucks." The purchaser reached into his pocket, took out a wad of one hundred-dollar bills, and peeled off ten of them. The dealer had one more demand, "Be sure to call me Friday morning and let me know if everything is the way you're telling me now. I don't want to bet my money then hear any lame excuses after the race."

Leaving the vehicle, he shouted, "No question. You will hear if something isn't right. What customer you got that is more dependable than Richie?" Sonny's facial expression said it all about his feelings "You ain't the one."

CHAPTER 11
Suzanne and Raymond Connect

Casually walking on her own to the training track, Suzanne, by chance, was slightly ahead of Raymond, who was also on a trip to the same destination. She hadn't seen him, so he quickened his pace to catch up while clearly calling out to her, "Suzanne, Suzanne, wait for me." Hearing and finally recognizing the voice, she slowed down and turned, greeting him with a pleasant smile, "Did not see you. Good morning."

Joining together, a conversation was started, but as they passed the next barn door, a riderless Thoroughbred with saddle and bridle in place, reins dangling came flying out of that stable toward them, creating an element of complete surprise and imminent danger! There wasn't any time to think! Zero! His only instinct was saving his secret love from the wildly running horse. Raymond embraced Suzanne wrapping both arms around her body, covering it with his own until they reached the ground. The trainer held the lady firmly, protectively, under him in a strong grip, as the spooked animal flew just inches over their bodies, covering them with clods of dirt.

When the danger was gone, he released the hold, but Suzanne would not soon, or ever, forget his sensuous embrace as she lay pressed against him. It was a timeless moment. The experience was surreal! Naturally being worried, it was necessary to quickly find out if Suzanne could stand. Offering a hand, she clutched it and managed to get up. His first question was "Are you alright?" Slightly dazed, she did not promptly answer, so the question was asked again, "Are you hurt?" Carefully, the woman gave her response, "I'm not sure." She shook her head several times, allowing her hair to swing from shoulder to shoulder.

Supporting the lady's effort to maintain balance, Raymond placed a hand on her waist, which was just the amount of helpful leverage that was needed. As they brushed themselves off, he removed Suzanne's scarf that was layered with dirt. Her senses were returning. "Let me catch my breath . . . What happened?" Describing the incident as the best it could he said, "A loose horse came out from nowhere, jumping over us, but we survived. That was close! That horse could have crushed us!" This was the time to be honest. "I never saw anything. Raymond, you saved my life. . . Oh My God! Thank you!" "If you had been hurt when with me . . . I would never, never have forgiven myself."

Still rubbing away dirt, she fully retained and valued that previous, incredible expression of concern for her safety. Most of all, being sincerely from his heart, it was obvious that he meant every word! "I think I'm still in one piece but should get back to the cottage by the barn and sit down to clear my head and freshen up." "Let me walk you there." "No, you go on . . . I'll be fine. You are busy." Brushing off more dirt, the lady became self-conscious. "Look at me. I must look awful."

Again, he spoke spontaneously and expressed his true feelings, "No, of course not. Never more beautiful!" This compliment deeply touched her. As Raymond gazed into her eyes, she could not help realizing that there was true sentiment in the words he spoke. The international translation in any language was I love you. Sadly, to express himself in any other meaningful way was not possible. Only his blue eyes could reveal his caring heart.

A crowd had gathered to assist them, so privacy did not exist. No matter, even if they were alone, it would have been impossible to come up with anything else deeply romantic. Enough intimacy, together time between them was lacking; he walked a fine line to remain proper. Although the lady suggested that he could leave her, he refused, "I couldn't let you walk back without me. Hold on to my arm for a little support." Showing himself to be caring, they walked side by side. There wasn't any resistance; she rested on his arm. As they slowly walked away, the fractious horse that jumped over them had been caught and was being led back to its barn. That Thoroughbred seemed no worse for the experience, but that surely added some excitement to its life.

Early the next morning, Raymond was in the shed row overseeing the training activities of his horses, getting a set ready to go out and train. The trainer had not thought of the previous day at that moment, but someone else did. A surprise visitor appeared. "Good morning, Raymond. How are you feeling today?" "Never better, Suzanne. And yourself?"

"Maybe a touch stiff, but nothing to worry about. I'm glad that you are here. Can you spare a minute?" "Anytime for you." Gently touching his arm, she spoke endearingly, "My family is hosting a charity benefit at our home on Saturday night, about 7:00 p.m. It's black tie. Could you possibly join us! This was the holy grail of invitations. "Yes, of course. I will look forward to that affair." Visually, she appeared pleased that the invitation was accepted so quickly. They chatted a few minutes, then Suzanne excused herself, knowing that the trainer was busy. Her mission was accomplished.

Seven- ten p.m. on Saturday night arrived. Raymond drove on a country lane until he reached a wide-opened black wrought iron gate with a golden letter B on its center. There, two off-duty police officers in dark blue suits professionally and politely checked the incoming arrivals against the printed guest list. Upon passing through that point, the trainer traveled less than a minute up a well-lighted, pine-tree-lined curved road to the top of a gently sloping hill. At the top majestically stood the main entrance of the ten-million dollar, twelve-thousand-square-foot, three-level redbrick Tudor Brockhurst mansion. Although a tour of the impressive home was not offered that evening, it shouted elegance. As he pulled up, it became obvious that his Mustang was overshadowed by limousines, Ferraris, and Mercedes with a scattering of Rolls and Bentleys parked on the massive lawn. The list goes on, but no one else had a Mustang.

Raymond, who usually had a good sense of humor was amused by that lopsided picture when trusting his sports car to the care of a female valet and requesting, tongue-in-cheek, "Take good care of my valuable car." She could appreciate his play on words. "Yes, sir. I will park it in the best spot and will make sure no one takes it by mistake."

Both laughed, he had been cleverly outsmarted and loved her comeback. Proceeding to reach the main entrance, a doorman opened one of the thick, nine-foot-high mahogany entry doors. That portal, a work of art, also had the large golden letter B classically inlaid into the center.

Once inside, a pleasant middle-aged woman, sitting alongside other ladies at a long glass table, offered a warm greeting. It gave the impression that she waited only for him. "Good evening, sir. Welcome to the Brockhurst home. Our pleasure to have you with us." "Good evening to you." "Your name, please?" "Raymond Masterson, a guest of—"

The clever aide graciously finished the sentence, "Oh yes, a guest of Ms. Brockhurst. She told us to expect a Mr. Masterson. Please, allow me to escort you to her." "Thanks for your kindness."

The attention given to him was impressive since he was certainly an unknown outsider among this prestigious group of socialites. Walking past the center of the ballroom that occupied the greater part of the main floor, he recognized the Brockhursts, Suzanne's parents. They were often seen at the races, with Raymond even saying, "Good afternoon, sir," to an engaged Mr. Brockhurst as they passed in the paddock. Perhaps his greeting was heard?

Isabel, a tall, shapely, elegant lady in her mid-fifties, was wearing a fashionable Channel black silk gown, a large white pearl necklace, and stylish middle heels, which made her slightly taller than her husband. The simplicity of the black color choice with the pearls was perfect for the complete outfit.

The gentleman, Charles, slightly older, was wearing a finely tailored Giorgio Armani tux, was in fit condition, and sporting a suntan, which gave him the appearance of an avid, serious golfer or a gentleman yacht owner. That impression was easily perceived, but under that disguise was a brilliant businessman. Although not wearing anything outlandish, their stature and central location made their couple's status self-evident, the king and queen of the ball.

Continually, as their guests came over to be acknowledged each was greeted as though they hadn't t been seen in years, even if the Brockhursts had lunched with them the day before. When the aide escorting Raymond walked near Charles and Isabel, she caught sight of him and asked her husband, "Charles, who is that fine-looking young man escorted by Jennie? I do not know him."

"That is Raymond Masterson, a trainer."

"Not the fellow who saved Suzanne's life?"

"Precisely so, dearest."

This information verbally excited the hostess. "Oh, I must meet him sooner than later. Can't wait. Suzanne said he would be here, but I did not know who to expect." Her husband carefully weighed his next words. "Do not be too anxious to waste your time with him. Let us not get too friendly. He is not Suzanne's type, and we don't want him hanging around here."

"Waste my time? Get friendly? How do you know Suzanne's type? Why would he want to hang out here? Dear, sometimes you confuse me." Shrugging his shoulders, he quickly turned, hoping to find someone new to greet. It was far easier than answering Isabel's barrage of questions. Continuing to their destination, Raymond was naturally unaware of the Brockhursts' conversation about him, particularly the negative aspects that haunted Charles. Jennie and he continued to walk through the crowded ballroom, which held over 150 guests. All the men were in tuxedos while the women wore gowns or evening dresses. A suit on a man or fashionable dress slacks on a woman could not be found.

This was the best of high society as reflected by those present. When he was brought to Suzanne's side, she greeted him as a friend with a casual, quick social hug. "Thank you for joining us." Then the trainer was introduced to her group, "Raymond, I would like you to meet my first cousin and closest friend, Ashley Montgomery. We grew up together."

"Hello, Ashley, a pleasure to meet you" The lady offered a hand and returned a vivacious, "Hello to you. I have heard so much about you from Suzanne. You are her hero! Welcome." That fanfare was not expected, therefore, Raymond had no way to verbally accept the acclaim. He looked to Suzanne, who seemed slightly embarrassed.

One of the other two men, frowning, was visually annoyed by that compliment. He appeared not comfortable to have Raymond joins their little private group with such a grandiose entrance. To this fellow, a hug and praise to anyone else, was unacceptable to his pride. A mind reader would interpret the unhappy man's thought as "Why is this fucking guy here?"

Turning to her other guests, Suzanne made the proper introductions. "Raymond, this is Paul McMillan and Jeff Rogers. You probably know of them." The trainer realized that Paul was Suzanne's morning companion the previous week at the racetrack, but at that time, he was too far away to be facially recognized. Now, he was meeting him in person along with his teammate. Jeff and Paul were two famous N F L players.

Eagerly shaking hands, he acknowledged them, "You are the two best receivers in the league. How do you make such great catches?" Jeff was appreciative of the compliment. "Loyal fan here. He doesn't remember the ones we dropped. You should come to all our games." All laughed except Paul, who still had a sour look on his face. He made no secret of the fact that, for some personal reason, Raymond wasn't worthy to be in such a select group, especially in his presence.

"Did you have any trouble getting here?" asked Suzanne "None at all. A half-hour drive and I received a great reception upon arriving. Paul was quickly tiring of the abundant attention he perceived that this newcomer was receiving, so he put his arm around Suzanne's waist, bringing her closer. Seeing an opening, the audacity to question her guest was seized upon, although he had been previously told the answer by the lady. The football player brazenly snapped, "Raymond, what is your game?"

The answer was straightforward without any hint of boasting, "I train racehorses." A sarcastic, demeaning remark followed, "How exciting. Any money in it?" Raised to be proper, Suzanne became uneasy upon hearing Paul's rude response and question, which was totally unacceptable anyplace, anytime.

Playing cool, he answered, "Never gave it much thought. I enjoy what I do. That's what is important to me." At this point, Paul gave Suzanne a "Ho-hum, where did you find this loser" look after Raymond had responded. That indiscretion of the athlete's question was observed by all, so the trainer decided that he might play the same game in a dignified way and pried. "Do you like what you do?" That question was taken as an insult, which it was meant to be, leaving Paul almost speechless. Nobody talked to him like this. He abruptly defended himself with a "Buddy, give it your best guess!"

The wide receiver only became more agitated, realizing that now was time to unquestionably exhibit a dominant male position, putting the trainer in his place, and ridding him of any intimate ideas regarding his woman. By design, he moved the large, strong hand that had rested on Suzanne's waist to her bare shoulder. Any observer would draw the same conclusion. Paul was obviously staking his claim on this beauty as private property! Strangers keep away or get shot! Reminding her, he said, "Sugar, you were going to take a walk with me in the gardens. I'm ready."

The proper lady was not allowing him to get his way with this. "Not now, Paul. Maybe later." It was not an acceptable response to what he asked. The big man put more pressure on Suzanne's shoulder, becoming vocally demanding, "Come on---Let's go---We need some fresh air" Experiencing discomfort and anxiety from Paul's hold, she gracefully slid away to be free.

During the elapsing time, a confused Raymond was trying to understand the dynamics of this strange situation. His eyes focused, and he thought that no one should ever touch a woman or speak to her in this way. Was it his proper place to say or do something? In this environment, he was uncertain, searching deeply inside himself for the right answer, which needed to be found fast! How could he ever expect his manhood to be challenged in such a manner by a professional football player, much less in a mansion crowded with high society people?

All Raymond's buttons had been pushed, creating an internal, sparking overloaded charge. Everyone in the group was tense, anticipating what the outcome would be. Something, someone had to give! The end of the road was reached! In a flash, Suzanne surprisingly saved the day. "I really must take Raymond to see my parents. They do want so much to meet him." Slowly, Raymond inhaled, the muscles in his body relaxed. Ashley and Jeff, who were standing on ground zero and were disturbed by the spectacle also felt relieved. All nodded in agreement to the proposal but Paul. There was little he could do. Suzanne had temporarily extinguished the fire of superiority and jealously in the stud. They left the group and went directly to her parents.

"Mom, Dad, I would like to introduce you to my friend, Raymond Masterson . . . Raymond, these are my loving parents, Charles and Isabel Brockhurst."

"A pleasure to meet you. I thank you both and Suzanne for the invitation to your home and this charity ball." Isabel assured him, "No, our pleasure. We are so pleased. It is a chance to personally thank you for protecting our daughter." In a somber tone, Charles added, "Yes, young man, really. A job well done."

Being humbly objective, Raymond replied, "Thank God, someone was there." It was more personal for Suzanne. "Thank God, it was you!" Charles was stone-faced, but with a natural knack to be inquisitive, Isabel had a gleam in her eye. She now had an open door to ask questions and have them all answered because this young trainer was a captive audience. "Raymond, tell me a little about yourself. Where you born in New York City?"

"No, Mrs. Brockhurst. In Brooklyn, Flatbush."

"You said that with some pride."

"Brooklyn is unique. It has its own soul."

Moving quickly into her next inquiry, she asked, "Now, what got you into training Thoroughbreds? There are only a few young men as yourself who are trainers, and they are sons of trainers." The reason was objective. "A long story longer than you would have time to hear, but more than not because I fell in love with Thoroughbreds at an early age. They are magnificent animals, and every day with them is an exciting challenge. No two days are the same. I can't wait to arrive at the barn in the morning."

Eager to add to the conversation was their daughter. "And Raymond is a good trainer. He needs more depth to his stable." Feeling left out of the loop, Charles chimed in, "Hang in there. Things have a funny way of turning around. His wife easily retook the spotlight, "I hope that we will be seeing more of you. There are so many things that I would like to talk about with you."

Soon it became necessary for Charles to give Isabel a slight stop-it poke in the back. Ignoring the signal, the lady smiled but was unstoppable in conversation. "Suzanne, why don't you introduce Raymond to some of our other guests. I am sure that they would love to meet him, and then be certain to bring him back later to talk with us." "A good idea, Mom. I will." Moving away, she shared a thought with him, "Now that you meet my parents. What do you think of them?" Here was another chance for the trainer to effortlessly become flattering. "Being your parents makes them special, and no one could ever claim that your mother is at a loss for words."

That comment was a plus. "An honest observation. They are special. I love them, and Mother is talkative, to say the least. Are you now ready for the other introductions or whatever?" She was hoping for whatever and her wish came through. "Yes, but could you first show me this fabulous garden?" These words were sweet to Suzanne's ear, a chance for them to be alone. "Sure. No one will miss us for a short time." The matter was settled. The garden it would be. They found their way through the crowd to the far- left side of the festive ballroom. After climbing down several classic white marble steps, they finally had reached the sheltered entrance to the outside garden.

Raymond and Suzanne simultaneously started intimate eye contact as they stepped onto the dimly lighted, solid carved field stone veranda where the ceiling was cradled by beautiful beamed gray oak boards. Three skylights captured stars in their frames that evening. Could this night, or would this night, turn out to be more than just a visit to a garden?

From this vantage point, there was a commanding view of the tastefully illuminated three-acre English garden surrounded by six-foot-high English laurel hedges. Throughout the gardens were small sparkling ponds. Each one was uniquely designed with a center fountain shooting water high into the air, returning quickly to splash, ripple, and play on the shimmering pond's surface before disappearing.

A variety of tall trees—white oaks, maples, and red cedars—made up most of the graceful giants with their leaves giving a symphony of colors, which distinguished the different seasons, leaving winter bare. There was no better time than that moment to venture into the splendor. At the foot of the veranda, there was a white gravel path that led to four others; the pair stepped down onto it, starting their fantasy journey.

Momentarily putting his garden observations on hold, Raymond initiated a light-hearted conversation with Suzanne, which he believed and hoped would help to bring them closer. "You are safer out here with me than you would be with Paul. Heck, any woman who goes out with him needs a bodyguard." Suzanne laughed. "I'm familiar with bodyguards." The comment ended there.

Allowing a few seconds of quiet to pass, Raymond was on edge to find out Suzanne's true feelings about wealth in an indirect way. He still strongly harbored a feeling of financial insecurity about their relationship. What did he have to offer her? She had everything twice. There was no question in Raymond's mind about how deeply he loved Suzanne but was her extravagant wealth going to be a burden, keeping them apart? If this lady at his side were penniless, his love would not be a question. What were Suzanne's deep feelings, foundations?

So, he ambitiously continued, praying for the right answer, "Didn't Paul just signed a three-year contract for two million?" "Yes, believe so . . . Lucky him." "I would have to win two lotteries to have that much money." "Money doesn't mean everything, and sometimes nothing." She well-remembered her time spent with the saintly sister. Raymond easily shared his thoughts on being rich. "I have always believed that, but I never had enough money to prove it."

Suzanne laughed yet wanted Raymond to feel comfortable with her realistic response about wealth. He became confident that at least money would never stand between them; however, her family's attitude was a different ballgame. Who knew?

Upon moving several yards further into the garden, Raymond started to really pay attention to this truly man- made paradise. Throughout the garden, ground lights were pointed into the trees for effect. Amazing landscapes held incredible floral design arrangements that could be considered works of art.

At specific areas, spotlights were changing colors to offer different visual tones to a visitor while golden moon slivers illuminated the edges of a few dark, low-flying clouds passing overhead. Fairyland effects prompted her quest to say, "I have never seen or experienced anything like this! Where are the leprechauns? This garden is enchanted." "That tells me something about your nature. You are an imaginative, sensitive person who can see and appreciate beauty."

He gave Suzanne his undivided attention with a double answer. It started with "I most certainly can appreciate beauty"—and ending with "Especially yours!" That was perfect! If this socialite had any inhibitions, they were gone. Raymond had hit a grand slam! When gently taking hold of the lady's soft hand, she willingly responded, tightening her grip. This gave Raymond a strong sense of oneness and warmth with the radiant woman at his side. They were both ready to express physically and verbally their basic inner desires. The trainer leaned over, placing a kiss on her ear; she promptly responded with one on his lips, then said softly, "Don't ever leave me. I love you."

The young lovers finally had broken down the wall of uncertainty that had separated them. Whispering into her ear, "You know that I have always loved you from the first time our eyes met" and was rewarded with several long, soulful kisses that embodied and expressed her passion. They embraced, holding each other tightly! The garden in which the two began their journey no longer existed unless you wanted to call it the Garden of Eden! Their original parents, Adam, and Eve, would have been proud of their children. Here was true love.

Reluctantly, after repeatedly committing to one another, they had to continue their walk. The real world still existed; return they must. Reaching the end of touring the garden, they entered the mansion by way of the same veranda. However, before that point, Raymond released her hand while holding Suzanne's arm in a nonromantic, formal way. They weren't desirous of creating any gossip; they sought to appear proper.

CHAPTER 12
Back to the Party

Once inside, Suzanne eagerly fulfilled the original task of introducing Raymond. She was precise in making certain that he met each of the families who owned racehorses. This did not go unnoticed by her father. He touched Isabel's elbow to get her attention. "Suzanne is introducing her guest to only our horse owner friends. What do you think of that?" That dilemma was easily solved. "My, my. What a clever daughter you have."

After completing her customized tour, she reluctantly realized the obligation to rejoin Ashley and the football players, hardly forgetting the tension that had been barely escaped. When they arrived, Paul's facial expression clearly showed that he was completely pissed off. He sternly addressed the socialite, "Where you been, princess?" Giving an honest answer in a low tone, she said, "Keeping busy. Moving about."

Again, in an unrelenting, commanding voice, he said, "I'm your date, and you left me! What's going on here?" This lady of breeding was not the confrontational type and tried to get by that comment without escalating the football player's rudeness and temper. "You are an honored, invited guest as are the others. I don't have a date with anyone."

Flipping his left hand high into the air, he said, "You and your new friend seem friendly enough. Maybe he's more honored. like a date!" Without warning, Paul started to aggressively advance in Raymond's direction, but the trainer firmly stood his ground. There were only several inches between their faces when Paul stopped and began speaking arrogantly while spraying saliva, "Maybe one of us should leave . . . now!

83

I don't play second fiddle to nobody . . . screw this setup. Nobody gets the best of me!"

There wasn't any response from Raymond while the other three were more than mortified. At that point, Paul gave Raymond an opened handed slap on the top of his shoulder. The trainer nobly kept his composure, didn't budge, didn't retaliate, but he also didn't want to imagine what was next. So far, he was a stationary target with no recourse!

This stud wasn't done; the same spot was hit again, deliberately harder this time with a closed fist. Jolted, Raymond found that standing motionless was impossible; the blow caused him to sway! Suzanne's guest, who now saw himself under an all-out attack, had no choice other than throwing both his fists simultaneously into Paul's lower ribcage as hard as he was able at that close distance The football player was far more furious than seriously hurt. He was now ready to unload on the trainer. Paul moved backward to set up his payback attack but accidentally banged solidly into large French doors behind him. This created a loud sound that echoed in the ballroom and caused most heads to turn in their direction.

At 6'4", 225 lb. Jeff, was equal to Paul in stature and strength, but the more sensible of the two. Immediately he realized the seriousness of the situation. He boldly thrust himself between the combatants, directly facing Paul. "Cool it, man. This ain't a offbeat bar! Let it go!" Paul's eyes and veins were bulging. One could wonder if Jeff's warnings were heard.

Standing firmly, Jeff was dead serious, repeating louder, "We don't want trouble. Let it go!" The aggressor drew several deep breaths and gave a loud snort. He knew the only way to beat up Raymond was to leap over his teammate, but there was no way that was going to happen in the real world. Paul had had it. "Let's get the fuck out of here!" Jeff couldn't have been happier. "Yeah. The sooner the better." As the players abruptly walked through the curious crowd, they ignored everyone.

People were staring, whispering, but they had no insight about what really occurred! Noticeably embarrassed was Suzanne. What a way to start a beautiful romance. What were all these special people in attendance going to think? Had she ruined her parent's party along with her newly chosen love life? Ashley's mouth was open. She couldn't grasp the unfolding event. For her, this was a gala affair; everyone should be happy, friendly, especially the athletes who were celebrities, known by all. What had happened? Guests continued to look in that direction where Suzanne stood.

Curiosity for them was difficult to dismiss. Human nature being as it is, they wanted to know what had caused this uproar. Why had the football players left in an inexplicable, rude rush? Repeatedly glancing at Raymond for support, Suzanne fully received the needed attention. Regrets, no excuses, were offered by Raymond. "For whatever I did wrong, I sincerely apologize."

"Paul has a big ego. That's not your fault, and he realized tonight wasn't his night or that this was the last time with me. His pride wouldn't accept that. Deciding to drop me whenever he chose would be his game, but the reverse was impossible."

"A lot happened, but I feel guilty. Maybe I should have gone home a long time ago when things started to get contentious, and this could all have been avoided. Anybody could have seen what was coming. The confrontation wasn't hard to predict. He wanted to fight from the beginning." Not wanting her lover to be upset, she said, "You were patient and acted properly. This is all my fault. I should have known what to expect. Paul cares only about himself. What happened here was inevitable. It was only a matter of time before the true man was revealed . . . Tonight was the night . . . Raymond, please put this incident out of your mind."

"Suzanne, I will . . . but I sincerely believe that now is time to call it a night. The sooner I leave here, the sooner people will forget about the disruption. That way, fewer questions for you to answer . . . This evening always shall be . . . unforgettable! What could ever match this?" Taking the nerve to move as close to her as he dared in public, Raymond spoke softly for only her ears to hear, he said, "My love is only for you." This was exactly what she needed to hear. She smiled then agreed with him about leaving. "I understand how you feel, but don't blame yourself. If you must go, at least let me walk with you to the entrance." While walking through the ballroom, all eyes were upon them, especially the eyes of an embarrassed and inquisitive Charles Brockhurst.

The host could not imagine what had happened. He was dumbfounded! Although they desperately desired to embrace, share a whole bunch of good-night kisses, and express their intimate thoughts in words to each other, they could not. The couple were center stage; there was no curtain to close!

CHAPTER 13
An Evil Visitor

Darkness had fallen. At the back of quiet barn # ten, a man could be found mixing in with the shadows. Gradually, the barn door was opened and from the dim, scattered overhead ceiling lights, Sonny's determined face came into view. The intruder hesitated, looked, and listened carefully to be certain that there was no one else in the stable. Wearing leather gloves, he finally walked in defiantly as if he owned the place to the first stall, swinging his agile body under the webbing. Holding that docile horse by its halter, he drew a wide ten-inch-long metal pipe from under his waistband and began slamming the poor, surprised horse twice on the knee. As the horse pulled back, it jerked the attacker's bent arm, which he shook several times in the air to offset the sting.

"Son of a bitch, dumb horse! Where are you going?" Spitting at the retreating animal, he threatened "You can't hide from Sonny!" As the terrified horse jumped awkwardly to a corner of the stall, Sonny, requiring vengeance, threw the lead pipe, hitting the already injured animal in the head just missing its left eye. Blood gushed! Satisfied with his work, the mauler moved to the next stall where he dropped the protective webbing. There was nothing there now to keep that Thoroughbred contained in the stall.

Moving to a third stall, he saw the lights of a racetrack security truck on patrol slowing down as it reached the far perimeter of the barn. The horses in barn # ten, sensing danger, were starting to act up, kicking, whinnying, and making other detectable noises. Sonny decided it was time to leave. He departed as stealthily as he arrived. The patrol truck continued to move because the driver never actually became aware of the brutality going on in the barn at that moment.

The horse in the unprotected stall pawed the straw for several minutes then pranced into the shed row. The Thoroughbred sought freedom as it jogged out past the sliding door left wide open by the gangster. Running over the cement road, its horseshoes created sparks, which were visible in the blackness of night. Upon reaching a fork in the road, the animal, at a full gallop, was not able to negotiate the sharp turn to the right, and fell onto the ground. It slid, ultimately crashing into a tree! Both front legs became twisted under its chest; blood began oozing out from beneath the animal's torn body. The injured horse, unable to move, lay helplessly traumatized.

A half hour later, another security guard in a vehicle was making the rounds when he discovered the injured horse. He immediately called the headquarters where Lieutenant Marigone, head of night security and a retired New York City detective, was located. "Base, pick up. There is a horse down on the road."

"Where . . . where are you?"

"Behind barn fourteen."

"Are any people hurt?"

"No one is here right now. Only me with the downed horse."

"I'll be there fast. Secure the area." In minutes the lieutenant arrived, trying to absorb and analyze the situation. He keyed his attention on the horse's halter: "What's the horse's name on the halter's nameplate?" The security guard bent over for a closer look. "Riptide. I know that horse. It belongs to Masterson. It raced only two days ago. This horse was a winner."

That information gave the lieutenant a starting point, and he wasted no time in giving an order. "Get Masterson fast and a vet even faster." At three ten a.m., Raymond was in a sound sleep at his one-bedroom apartment located in Rockville Center, Long Island, New York. He had been up at four thirty a.m. the previous morning, gone to the barn to train then spent that afternoon at the races with clients. As early evening on that day approached, there was just enough time to return home, shower, change into his rented tux, reaching the ball at the Brockhurst's mansion, close to the time Suzanne had suggested.

When he put his head on the pillow at eleven-thirty p.m., he had nearly been awake continuously for twenty hours, and Raymond was exhausted. The tux, shirt, and bow tie that were worn to the ball were thrown on a bedside chair, and the still shined black shoes were on their sides under the bed, which had waited for their return. His socks were still on. The trainer's phone rang and rang. Slowly he sat up, bewilderedly answering it, wondering who could be calling at this hour. "What! What! No! Are you sure it is my horse?" "Riptide. Yes, I train him. I'll be right there!" He quickly threw on cloths and ran out to his car.

While driving sleep-deprived, his body could at best only generate a twinge of numbness while the same thought continually ran through his mind, "How did my horse get loose? How did my horse get loose?" When Raymond pulled up, there stood the security men and some grooms, who were awakened by the arrivals of vehicles. They gathered in silence at the motionless horse's side in an area eerily illuminated by the security's truck's lights.

One of Lieutenant Marigone's staff, a horse lover, was upset, besides himself; however, he was the person nearest to the trainer as Raymond stepped out of his car. Mustering the courage to speak, the information available was offered, "Mr. Masterson...somehow, he got loose. I found him this way. I'm awfully sorry. This was a terrible thing to have called you about." The grief-stricken horseman responded, "Thanks for feeling way . . . Did someone call a vet? This poor horse needs a vet!" He desperately called out for reassurance, "Is a vet coming?" The security driver affirmed, "Yes, sir. I did call. One should be here soon."

Staring at his fallen horse, Raymond instinctively dropped to his knees, gently rubbing its head the same tender way he had rubbed the heads of the mares in Vineland, New Jersey. Tears started to form under the trainer's eyes, running down his cheek. They were pushed away with the back of his hand but to no avail. New and bigger ones took their place immediately.

"Why? How did this happen." The trainer was questioning, blaming himself Shortly thereafter, the on-call vet arrived. Fortunately, it was

Raymond's vet, Dr. Matthews. There was only one comment to make, "Doc, this is bad." Raymond never looked up, only down at the injured Thoroughbred as he spoke,

"What do you think?" Using a powerful flashlight, Dr. Matthews squatted down to examine the animal. He negatively shook his head and after a short examination said, "Not good. This animal doesn't have a chance in the world. Both front legs are broken. Got to put him down."

The tears had increased under Raymond's eyes, running down the full length of his sullen cheeks and falling onto the opened blue shirt, "Doc, do what it is fast. This horse has suffered enough." The vet went quickly to his vehicle, promptly returned, and injected a yellowish substance directly into the horse's jugular vein. The animal's whole body quivered then became motionless. The agony was over! The bystanders, horse-loving backstretch employees, had looked the other way as the euthanasia was administered.

Raymond continued to rub the Thoroughbred's head with both his hands even after it had expired. This horse was his responsibility; it was dead, and this trainer endured the unbearable pain of self-imposed guilt! The lieutenant asserted his authority; he wanted to investigate. "Let's go back to your barn and see if we can make any sense of what happened. I have never seen a racehorse in such a terrible condition and don't ever want to see it again."

Walking into the barn, Raymond sadly became aware of the injured horse in the first stall; it was in obvious distress. He alerted the vet, "Doc, come here. A horse is hurt." The doctor turned around to see what Raymond was alluding to. "Yes, you are right." After entering the stall, he examined the animal. "Some unusual marks on the knee, which is already swollen and a deep wound on the head; near its eye." The pipe lying on the straw drew Raymond's attention. "And there is the reason."

Lieutenant Marigone cautioned, "Don't touch it. Maybe it has prints." He found a towel, loosely placed the pipe on it, and then handed it to one of his security personnel, "Lock this in the glove compartment." The injured animal was evaluated by the vet. "I'll stitch up her head wound, give her antibiotic, tetanus, and some bute to kill the pain. We can have the knee X-rayed in the morning."

"That all sounds for the best. Doc, thank you for being on call. This isn't an easy night for anyone." Firmly, the veterinarian placed his right hand on Raymond's upper arm as a gesture of his full understanding of the circumstances while sharing the trainer's grief.

Raymond stared at the hanging webbing in the front of the next stall, which was there to keep the animal safe inside. "A horse can't open that on its own. What kind of lowlife could do this to a helpless animal?" The puzzled security people looked at each other. They had no answer.

At that point, Dr. Matthews pulled Raymond off to the side. Speaking in a low but firm tone, he said, "We damn well know who did it. What are you going to do? Maybe it is the right time to tell them about the gangsters?" The trainer was not convinced. "Not yet. It wouldn't do any good. Still no proof . . . Nothing can be done. Maybe talking about our friends tonight would make things worse." Dr. Matthews hesitated, trying to understand that point. "I guess that you are right, but I'm not sure. What a spot to be in. If you were ever looking for a damned if you do or damned if you don't, this will fit the bill."

There was one wishful hope remaining for Raymond to share, "Maybe Lady Justice will show her face." In the back of the young man's mind came a sobering thought, had Uncle Vito's efforts to help failed? Was this a mountain that he couldn't be climb? Had the trainer always been on his own? He would never be told or able to find out that Vito had used all his power and cunning to save his life! Any other concession was not possible!

Uncle Vito, who could do no more, would never talk about his connection with Tommy Z or his own deep personal involvement. The godfather's best cards were played. He was all-in, trying to keep his nephew safe! That was the only concession that Tommy Z personally acknowledged. Retribution was not taken off the table; he could not completely walk away from the cries of his mob for vengeance. Vito understood that mentality and could do nothing to stop it. Raymond, who was totally confused by the dynamics of this underworld situation, felt alone. Where could he turn? He had already gone once to Vito; twice was out of the question.

<h1 style="text-align:center">CHAPTER 14
Suzanne Comforts</h1>

*I*t was the crack of dawn as a silver-gray Porsche 911 Turbo pulled up at Raymond's barn. Charles had made his daughter aware of the incident, and as soon as she knew, Suzanne was compelled to be at her lover's side as quickly as possible. Gracefully stepping out of her fancy sports car, Suzanne searched for Raymond, and when together, she gave him a long consoling hug. "Oh, Raymond, what can I say? What is wrong?" Still visibly shaken, Raymond tried to pull himself together. He spoke in a low, broken, tense voice, "The poor animals never had a chance . . . If I could have been here, I could have saved them." "Don't blame yourself. Who did this?"

"It would be impossible to prove who was here. No witnesses. This happened in the middle of the night." "What in the world are you going to do? It worries me. You are vulnerable." Hesitating for a second, he said, "There is only one option. I can't be here twenty-four hours a day, so I'll have to put on a night watchman. It will be expensive, but that will keep the horses safe."

"It should." Her emotions were overflowing. "But I am still at loss for the right words to comfort you. This is terrible! I want to help. Tell me how? Please, let me help you."

"You don't have to do anything. Your companionship is what I need . . . always feel happy when you are near me . . . the nearer the better. Your touch and love are my strength. Sweetheart, having you here at this moment doesn't allow me to feel lost. Love is deeper than despair."

"Allow my love to always be in your heart. Then, this problem, whatever it is must be solved by you." Suzanne departed after she kissed him. That same afternoon, the trainer was again in a familiar part of the paddock area, getting a horse saddled for the fifth race. As he glanced at the crowd surrounding him, Sonny's face boldly stood out; it spoke defiance.

The gangster projected a shit-eating grin, which caused Raymond to be beside himself. He tried to control his anger by firmly placing his forehead against the strong neck of the horse that he was saddling. Visibly, forcefully, this trainer was concentrating on control, fighting the storm of rage within! Revenge, revenge was the only thought on his mind! A thin wall of logic held him back.

By jumping over the four-foot wrought iron fence that separated the saddling area from the patrons and attacking Sonny, the trainer would become the aggressor and the scum viewed as a victim. The charges against him would lead to legal and professional suicide, and besides, he couldn't give Sonny, a hardened killer, much of a fight. Did it need to be proven again how tough the enforcer was? The mental frustration was brutal!

The valet sensed that the saddling rhythm wasn't there and became inquisitive, "Ray, where are you? Let's get this one saddled." The trainer could barely speak, "Will ya give me . . . give me a second." After a moment, the distressed man, as best as he could, again gave his full attention to saddling, but his hands were uncontrollably shaking, physically expressing the wild feelings that were running through his mind and body!

Not a violent man by nature, evil thoughts consumed his soul. He wanted to kill Sonny! The power of this emotional storm was unbearable. He was out of control and fighting his inner self's turmoil by holding on to a frail level of rationality. Sonny's brass balls presented an untenable challenge! Luckily, inexplicably, he was blessed with the strength needed, never again looking to see Sonny's whereabouts. Had he seen the degenerate still there taunting and glaring at him, Raymond would have lost it no matter the consequences. His honor demanded it; his sense of justice screamed for retribution!

Far surpassing its breaking point, Raymond's spirit had exploded! Upon later reflection of this event, Raymond said a prayer of thanks. He had been saved from self-destruction. The horse in that race hadn't run particularly well, but larger problems occupied his thoughts as he exited the track. The next morning, the couple were together again for coffee; the sign outside the cozy backstretch restaurant read, "Lily's Kitchen— Where the Best Meet . . . the Best Eat!" A small notice on the side of the door stated, - Private Restaurant - Restricted: - Owners - -Trainers - - Jockeys and Agents - - Track management - This restaurant had an L-shaped counter with eight high stools and six small tables in the open area; this eatery was solely for those listed above. The couple sat at a two-seat table by the wall, each holding a piping hot coffee while sharing a donut cut in half.

Meanwhile, Lily, a heavyset, short black lady in her mid- sixties, moved about while chatting with her customers. In her right hand, she carried a miniature jockey's whip with which she taped her favorites for that day on the shoulder. Lily acted as a queen knighting her chosen ones. The patrons loved the impromptu ceremony. Reaching the young couple's table the owner lamented, "Heard what happened at your barn. What is this world coming to?"

"I'm fighting the battle. You know how it goes." Suzanne reassured, "Raymond will work it out. I am certain." Changing the subject matter, the trainer asked, "Is our gracious hostess doing well?" "Every day I'm here with my three sisters operating this restaurant. Great sisters, fine customers. I'm a busy and happy lady. Could there be more?" "Congratulations. You have life going your way," said an admiring Suzanne. Scanning the table, Lily noticed the donut cut in half. "If everybody ordered like that, I would be out of business fast." The lady offered an explanation, "We are watching our figures." "Ms. Brockhurst honey, everybody's watching your figure." With some of his sense of humor still alive, Raymond joked, "Anyone watching mine?"

"Lily is, but maybe I'm the only one." The comment brought a needed laugh. "You both need to eat more. I serve the best." The trainer verified by saying, "Lily, if you put a rock on your grill, it would taste delicious."

"Thank you. Could you put that in writing?" The owner scanned the other tables, starting to realize that she may be overstaying her visit with them. "I've been here too long. Time for me to leave." Again, the proprietor looked at the donut and laughed. In a caring manner, Suzanne touched his face with both hands then studied her lover's eyes, asking him, "Raymond, you look tired. Did you get any sleep?"

"No." Too many things are going wrong, a horse hurt and another killed, plus I already lost an account. Mr. Cox didn't feel comfortable leaving his horses in my barn. He owned the injured filly. He is a horse lover, and what happened was heartbreaking. Who could blame him? The other owners are staying with me, at least for the time being. They believe that a night watchman on duty will prevent this from occurring again." Raymond took a swallow of coffee and finished his half of the donut. "There is more. My horses are in great condition but running awfully, and I'm using some of the best jockeys, Juan, Jose, and Carlos.

What's wrong? How true when he said I would be in hell? You can understand how all this confusion makes my sleeping difficult." Suzanne seemed puzzled by that last powerful comment and jumped on it. "Who said what about-- hell?" The trainer quickly realized that, unintentionally, too much of his secret life was revealed. Bruno's name and any of his threats should never come to her ears. "It's just an old expression. Don't pay attention to it."

The lady did not understand the answer but decided to question no more. Tapping the table with her long fingers, she let her thoughts escape, saying, "Raymond, let me change your luck!" "Do you have a fairy godmother or a rabbit's foot? I'm not going to be choosey . . . Whatever works is fine."

"Neither, much better . . . Train for me. I am very lucky!"

"But you don't own any horses."

"Easy. We can buy one at an upcoming auction . . . What do you think?"

"Suzanne, are you sure about this?"

"Certainly . . . Do you consider yourself a gambler on life?"

"Yes, that I'm sitting here with you proves that everything is possible . . ."

"A gambler always believes that he has a chance . . . Go for it!" was her encouraging response. Suzanne's beautiful, inviting eyes expressed hope. The trainer still was at a momentary loss for words, regained his composure, and declared, "This kind of proposition goes beyond any expectation. It is more than considerate. This is wild, and I appreciate the idea to train for you." Raymond leaned across the table. "I love you, and you are crazy---crazy!" A new partnership was formed, and an adventurous one it was destined to be. There was a sale of yearlings being held in Kentucky, and that was where they traveled to find the impossible dream.

Potential buyers flowed from barn to barn while looking for purchasable prospects on which to bid. A Thoroughbred sale was a place set in a time where all aspirations were possible. Negative thoughts were not allowed. When those in attendance selected a horse to examine, it was brought out from its stall for their inspection. Buyers made notes in their sales catalogs on what they deemed noteworthy or undesirable on each individual animal that was chosen.

The consignors usually had favorable, interesting stories attached to many of the horses they were selling. This was a buyer-beware situation. It was important to realize they were buying a racing prospect, not a story. Although varying degrees of skills encompass the individual buyers, there were some basic guidelines they all followed. A racehorse's conformation and breeding are at the top of that list, then comes the purchase's personal preference of a certain type of horse—are they seeking a sprinter or a distance runner, perhaps a turf horse rather than a main track competitor? Would a filly be better in their stable makeup instead of a colt?

The bottom line to all those critical factors is money. How much is that animal going to fetch and how much cash do they have in their checking account? So a buyer can understand that even for the most astute bidder, getting what they want was not an easy task, and there were not any guarantees of a successful purchase before or after the fact, only hope.

This ritual was repeated countless times, usually starting several days to a week before the actual sale began. By sales time, potential buyers believed that they had done their proper homework, and were ready to spend their money. Near capacity, this pavilion could hold about four hundred people, seated. Two auctioneers manned the podium while five, who also took bids, were stationed at different parts of the seating area. One was placed outside the structure in a designated place where a limited number of sales horses assembled before entering the ring.

Placing themselves in the middle of the pavilion, near the front, they waited for the horse that they had selected to enter the sales ring. It was timed, so the wait and tension would be short-lived. The trainer casually recalled their several days of efforts. "We sure have checked out a lot of horses. My feet hurt." With a half nod, she agreed, "But the one coming next into the sales ring is the one, the only one that we really want!" That statement was right on. "Yes. There is no doubt that colt is our top choice by a mile. I hope the bidding doesn't get out of reach." They held their breath as hip number 312 was brought into the ring. Suzanne sighed, "There he is . . ."

A strapping, shinning chestnut yearling colt, sixteen hands high with two white hind stockings was led into the ring. His powerful shoulders, muscular hindquarters, and overall conformation bode well for him. He greeted the bidders with several deep whinnies, surveyed the surroundings, and made sure that he gave the crowd a spirited kick with his right hind leg. This colt made certain everyone knew that he had arrived and was paying attention! The auctioneer began the bidding "Let's start this good-looking colt by the young sire, Devan, out of the stakes-winning mare, Utopia, at $300,000 . . . Do I hear $300,000 . . ."

He waited. There wasn't any audience response. He started again, "Do I hear $250,000 . . . Let's get started then at $ 250,000 . . . Let me hear $250 . . . 250!" A hand went up. "OK. Now $ 300,000 . . . I need $300,000 . . . A steal at $300,000." Another hand raised. "Who will gimme $350,000 . . . $ 350,000?" Not hesitating, Suzanne waved her left hand excitedly, offering "$350 thousand!" At that instance, her heart skipped a beat. She had declared herself! Her secret emotions were no longer private; they were thrown into the sales ring!

Looking in the direction of the previous bidder, the auctioneer cried out, "Let's not get cheap now . . . Gimme $375,000 . . . $375 . . . Worth $ 375 . . . Take a good look at this exceptional colt. Don't lose him."

Holding her breath, Suzanne waited to see if the bidding was about to escalate! Was she in a strong position or about to be outbidded? If another offer came, then what? Should she go higher? That decision would be based on her personal judgment, not a financial consideration. Few in the pavilion could challenge her ability to continue bidding. There was a silence, a forever silence; no other hand had yet waved. The auctioneer scanned the pavilion, giving his bid takers a final check, he was searching for one more explosive bid. Finally, he held the gavel high in the air. "Last call . . . Going once . . . Going twice . . . Gone!

Sold to the pretty lady upfront." A deserving hug was given to Suzanne by her lover, whose heart was also beating double time. "Congratulations. You got him. Wow!" Casually, he asked, "How high would you have gone?" "That is for me to know. Don't be nosey . . . Isn't he gorgeous? I love him!" Summing it up, Raymond declared, "This colt sure looks the part. He is textbook perfect. Thank you." They kept on admiring the colt as he left the sales ring. Their dreams for the future knew no boundaries.

They returned to the sales stable area to give this Thoroughbred a formal welcome. Suzanne caressed his neck and massaged it while Raymond rubbed the horse's muzzle. The lady stepped back, reaching into her purse, from which she drew three circular red-and-white peppermint candies. They were offered one at a time, and the colt made them disappear rapidly. She and her new purchase hit it off from the start.

Returning to their hotel, they sat side by side in a plush leather booth. It was evening time at the main dining room of Tri-City Hotel where others, who had come for the sale, were also at tables. Even if you didn't know them by name, the sales catalogs by the sides of their plates gave them away as horse buyers. There was a typical question to be asked of the owner, "Suzanne, have you chosen a name for your new purchase?" Without hesitation, she revealed the name, "A Sure Thing."

"I like it. What was your reason for that choice?"

"Because it was what we both need!" The trainer fully understood the depth of that remark for himself. "Truer words were never spoken. During the time of the injured horses and the other problems, I was stopped dead at a wall, desperate . . .almost out of business. I felt alone. How did my troubling time relate to you?"

"I was right at your side!"

"This isn't fair," said Raymond in a soft tone. "You are making me love you more, and I didn't think that was possible!" Suzanne paused, touched Raymond's arm. "Remember this. I believe . . . love has no limits." She then gave him a kiss. The young couple was nearing the end of dinner as Suzanne covered a yawn. "I am exhausted." Raymond could not agree more. "We looked at over seventy-five horses yet had everything riding on one. That effort and the pressure would tire anyone. We should call it an early night." She openly yawned. "No argument from me."

The conversation between them came to a temporary halt, but they held each other's hand with tenderness. Raymond leaned over, whispering something into her ear. Suzanne laughed, trying to cover it up by placing the back of her hand against her mouth. Any observer would sense that this couple was deeply in love, a volcano ready to erupt!

After dinner, they went through the lobby, took the elevator to the fifth floor where, outside of her room #510, she turned to Raymond, putting her head on his chest. He completely fascinated, embraced Suzanne. She sighed deeply, placing her arms around his neck while murmuring, "I will sleep well tonight." A soft, warm kiss to his lips followed. Raymond could not contain himself; there was a better alternative, "Bet you would sleep soundly in my arms."

"No doubt, but I might fall asleep quickly." A simple solution presented itself, "Should we gamble on it?"

"Yes," said the lady. "It is just the right time to gamble on love!"

Taking her key, Raymond opened the door while putting his arm around the woman he cherished. They entered arm in arm as the door was gently closed behind them. Moments after, it opened abruptly; it appeared as though Suzanne was leaving, but, she was playfully placing the "Do Not Disturb" sign on the outside handle. Everything was under control! These lovers were ready to make a lifelong commitment!

CHAPTER 15
Father and Daughter

Behind the Brockhurst mansion was an elaborate stable with a nearby ten-acre polo field that covered a manicured pasture. A Hollywood movie could be filmed there. Dew was on the morning grass as a ponytailed Suzanne guided a jumper over hurdle after hurdle. Tight white jodhpurs revealed her femininity. She was poetry in motion, nothing less. Suzanne was a beautiful, vivacious, talented equestrian.

As the rider returned to the barn, a female groom greeted her and held the reins, allowing Suzanne to comfortably dismount. The handler then brought the lathered horse inside to a washing area for a bath. Turning away from her mount, the rider noticed that her father's Rolls Royce was parked on the grass alongside a fence. It was unusual for him to be there at this hour of the morning because, normally, he was already early into his business activities, which didn't allow him free time.

Opening the car door, Charles strutted over to his daughter. "Good morning, my dear. Did you enjoy your ride?" "This horse is so perfect. No mistakes. I am so happy to have him." Looking first up at the sky then to his daughter, it was evident by the sweat on his brow that something was troubling this man. Eventually, he glanced downward and rubbed his forehead with the back of his hand. It was imperative for him to organize his thoughts, presenting them properly because the content of this conversation had to be effective right away; there was not a second chance.

Certain of that, his inquiry commenced, "Suzanne, you bought an expensive colt the other day, and I found out you are not giving it to our trainer. Why? I am truly confused and embarrassed." "Dad, there is no reason to think that way. I can make correct choices about what I want. Having a Thoroughbred with Raymond was my own decision. That was my only reason for purchasing the colt."

He rubbed his forehead once again, this time with a handkerchief. "I do not know you anymore, spending so much time with that trainer and doing unpredictable things. What about Paul? You were with him for several months. It seemed serious and now no more. What happened?" The daughter maintained her composure. "It was an unfortunate Mistake. Paul is not for me. Never really was. I enjoy Raymond's company. Truthfully, Dad, he is many times the man Paul is or ever will be." This was not the response Charles desired. "Don't get too involved with the trainer. His background is unknown, at best, nondescript."

"Sorry. It is too late."

"It is never too late! Your mother and I only want the best for you. You realize that." "Of course, I know. But remember, Raymond risked his life to save mine. He is a genuine person. Dad, trust me. Does that have any meaning? Can you plain trust me?"

"Certainly, he has courage. I cannot deny him that. However, it does not mean you have to be at his side indefinitely or feel any obligation to him. We can give him money. If necessary, a lot of money to disappear. Compensation and gone go together. You will be free." Straining to hold her composure, she said, "Money owed for services rendered or my sense of loyalty are not holding me to him. I want to be with him. Give the fellow a chance. He shall prove himself in other ways to you. Raymond is special! Do you know he has never discussed the events of the morning that he saved me. Never!"

"Perhaps he is smart enough to let it sit, thereby getting the most possible sentimental value from the situation out of you."

"Dad, you are right. He cannot wait to jump in front of another horse and show me how brave he is!" Soon her father reached the strongest point of this lecture: "Enough conversation. Suzanne, face the facts. This trainer is in a completely different social circle than us, a rank outsider! What could he possibly give you?"

"What every woman wants . . . love!" Charles had not succeeded; another course must be taken. The walls of their second-floor library had all its bookshelves crowded with no gaps. A complete array of books was an easy task, for one of the organizations in Charles's conglomerate was the Brockhurst Publishing Company.

He and Isabel rested there with reclining leather chairs underneath them. On the table between, stood a bottle of Louie XIII with two empty crystal glasses, no ice, and waiting to be filled. The couple was comfortable with the mood being set for a long conversation. The master of the house began, "Isabel, what are we going to do about Suzanne? What would you suggest?" Seconds passed but no answer was volunteered, so he eagerly continued, "She is foolishly involved with that run-of-the-mill trainer, blinded by love, or what our child thinks that word means. We know it is plain folly." Profound advice followed from Isabel, "Love is not easy to find . . . How many romances fall apart . . . bad advice . . . bad situations? True love is precious! Perhaps our daughter has found it."

Shaking his head, Charles wanted Isabel to agree with him. "Do not confuse the issue. Suzanne needs someone of substance, the right kind of man. She cannot love . . . a nobody!"

"Come on, Charles. Wake up. Suzanne knows her own mind. She is quite capable of making that personal commitment."

"You are surer than I am. That football player was the type of man for her. Famous, good earning power, handsome, strong . . . Need I go on?" Again, came a different viewpoint from a wise mother. "And if they got married? How many nights would he be at home? Before Suzanne, his toys included a cover girl, an actress, and some others who's private, personal lives were so uninteresting that they never got into the rumor mills of gossip columns."

Making light of her observation, he said, "All men have to sow their oats. He would have seen our Suzanne in a different light." Wound up, the wife would not let up. "That one is an addicted playboy. Paul is the type who will never stop. Oh yes! You can be certain that he would lead a comfortable life when no longer able to play football with our daughter filling the checkbook . . . If I wasn't a lady, I would call him . . . a bum!"

Immediately, Charles sought a different path to follow. "Alright, alright. Maybe . . . Paul was a bad example, but our genuine, close wealthy friends have sons, that are substantial, proud in their own rights, well-connected, superbly educated in Harvard, Princeton, or Yale. Why not . . . one of them?"

"Ask Suzanne. How should I know?" "Maybe being friends with most of them since her youth. She clearly sees their faults—pride, greed, insensitivity, or whatever!"

"There has to be a solution to stop this budding romance. I still control your mother's inheritance to her of seven million dollars, not to be dispersed until she turns twenty-two. Maybe I should become stricter, a lot stricter. I believe that time has come. What do you think?"

"Charles, your daughter loves you. Do not create an avoidable problem. Anyway, if she ever needed money, no matter the amount, I would give it."

"Please, Isabel, I am desperate to make her see the light."

"You mean your light!" No longer being able to think clearly, he said, "Woman, I can never win an argument with you?" A slight sigh emanated from the imperturbable lady. "Keep trying!"

CHAPTER 16
Developing a Racehorse

"A Sure Thing" was a Thoroughbred ready to develop his talents. After purchasing the colt in November, as a yearling, it was sent to a training center in Ocala, Florida, for five months It would be broken in and taught the basic steps before being sent to the racetrack.

Their sales purchase was instructed to accept the saddle and bridle. He then began initial training with leisurely gallops in company with other horses. The colt showed above-average intelligence from the beginning while he eagerly put his all into the morning training sessions. In early April, after learning the required lessons taught at the Ocala Training center, the colt was sent to the racetrack. Raymond was now ready to introduce the two- year- old into the real world of Thoroughbred training. Under Raymond's guidance, as the weeks passed, the galloping distances increased in length and speed as "A Sure Thing" matured."

During a Thoroughbred's life at the track, the most important factors in its day-to-day existence are soundness, fitness, and keeping it happy. Placing these qualities, or better said, bringing them out of a racehorse required a certain skill, which was the domain of a trainer. During morning training, clocked workouts initiated at the trainer's discretion eventually allowed a horse to build up racing speed with stamina. Following weeks of long gallops, trainers usually began the serious development with a workout of a one-quarter mile in twenty -six seconds, which gradually increased with quickness and distance.

At the track, development takes several months of planned and patient scheduling to realize a finished product. Part of this program included overcoming setbacks, which were always inevitable. It could be a fever, a swollen ankle, or some muscle soreness. After the training program was completed, the Thoroughbred became ready to do what he was bred for, to race. It was during training hours on a sunny morning as Raymond and Suzanne were waiting outside the barn when Jockey Steve Kelly arrived.

"Good morning, Ms. Brockhurst, Ray."

They replied in unison, "Good morning." Requesting for orders, Kelly asked, "Ray, what's on the work tab for today?"

"Take him to the starting gate and work five-eighths of a mile in a minute. That will be his last workout before a race, and I need to get the okay card from the starting gate crew to enter him." The objective was understood. "That should be easy. He has been there enough times and showed sense."

The colt, who had been walking around the shed row was brought onto the horse path where the jockey got a leg up on his mount. Waiting was a rider, a pony boy on a horse, who would escort "A Sure Thing" to the gate and keep him company on the return to his barn. A companion animal has a settling effect on the more highly explosive Thoroughbred.

They are used sometimes during morning training hours but almost always at race time going to the post. Trainers did not want to get their jockey exhausted in the post-race warmup, trying to get an excited racehorse to settle down or, even worse, have the animal run off! If a horse becomes uncontrollable and runs once around the track in the post-race gallop, it is automatically scratched from the race by the stewards.

The young couple walked to the track, positioning themselves across from where the starting gate stood. This gave them the proper angle from which to time the workout. They watched as their charge was loaded into the gate with three other horses who were also breaking. They may have been other two-year- old's or possibly older, experienced runners. The mix is up to chance. Their stopwatches were at the ready. Suzanne looked at hers then at the gate. "I hope my timing will match yours." "It will. Anyway, a one-fifth of a second either way doesn't mean anything."

They were keen on catching the break. The first call came from Suzanne. "He is out of there!" Both clicked their stopwatches, and after the first quarter, they took a split, which is a part of the total time. Raymond noted, "twenty-four." She compared. "Twenty- four and a one- fifth." As the colt reached the five- furlong marker, they clicked again. The owner was first to state her findings, "Five- eighths of a mile in fifty-nine seconds. Not a minute as we expected. Why can I not get it right?"

"No. If you were wrong, then so am I. My watch shows the same time, and he was going much faster at the end than at the start. What a terrific move."

Back at the barn, they eagerly waited for the horse and jockey to return. As Steve dismounted, Raymond couldn't wait to speak to him, "Steve, we got you in fifty-nine seconds flat!" Casually dropping the reins on the horse's neck, he said, "Don't let that stopwatch fool you. I had to hold him all the way. Your colt could've worked in fifty-seven easily if I let him. You got a runner here."

What a way to start a day! The couple was elated, and Raymond got a hug then another. With any encouragement he could have had embraces all day. Wednesday of the next week, the second race, and a group of two-year-old's circled around the paddock, mostly first-time starters. They showed their vigor, curiosity, and lack of racing experience. Of the eight, one in particular, "Greek Chief," reared up and unseated its jockey as soon as he got aboard. Luckily, the groom did not lose control of his charge, and the trainer, in short order, remounted that rider.

Raymond observed how mature his entry behaved. He acted as though he had been there many times before, which was always a good sign for a first-time starter. A nervous, lathered animal at any time would indicate that valuable energy is being wasted prior to the race, and that will affect performance. They watched him attentively until he strutted through the tunnel that led to the racetrack. While the horses were on the track, beginning to warm up, the duo moved to the box area, and with binoculars around their necks, they observed the field of starters warming up.

The gangsters sitting in a nearby box, smoked cigars while reading their racing paper. Occasionally, they deliberately and obnoxiously glanced over. Their stares caught Raymond's attention, but to Suzanne, they didn't exist and she didn't have any reason to look in that direction.

"Well, good luck," commented Raymond. "Our first race together." The track announcer took over. It was post time. "The horses were loaded into the starting gate . . . They are set. They're off." Both raised their binoculars, watching as "A Sure Thing" flew out of the gate to a quick lead.

The trainer made a verbal observation, "In front by three and the race just began. He is fast out of the gate!" Announcer: "As they run down the backside, "A Sure Thing" is now in front by five lengths; "Manitoba," second; "Allure," third; By "Partisan," fourth; "Joe Boy", fifth, "Greek Chief," sixth, trailing far behind them."

"I'm enjoying every second of this!" said Suzanne. Although however excited the pair were inside, they stood as still as statues, holding their binoculars steadily. Announcer: "The horses hit the three-eight pole and no change in the order. "A Sure Thing" is having it his own way. No challenges yet." Amazed, the owner exclaimed, "This looks too easy." She felt comfortable enough to put down her binoculars, holding on to Raymond's arm. Victory seemed assured. Announcer: "They're coming through the stretch. The leader in front by ten lengths. The only part of this race to still be decided is for second money."

"A winner first time out. You are as lucky as you said."

"What a thrill, watching my very own horse win."

The gracious lady, who would never forget this day, wanted to show simple appreciation, "Thank you."

"Really, the thank you is to you. It was your decision that made this happen."

Announcer: "A Sure Thing," first; "Partisan," second; "Joe's Boy," third; and "Greek Chief" up for fourth. The time three-quarters of a mile in 1 minute, ten and two-fifths seconds." Jumping up and down in ecstasy, they embraced one another. Still taking it all in was the Bruno-Sonny team, but they did not share in the same celebratory sentiment. Their look of disgust would create chills in anyone!

The thrilled couple found their way to the winner's circle for their first memorable photo together. The trainer spoke to the jockey. "Congratulations." "He did it all on his own. I never had to urge him." The jockey repeated a previous observation, "Ray, this horse got class. He is a runner."

CHAPTER 17
Ladies Chatting

Waiting amid the surroundings of an upscale bistro, located on the North Shore of Long Island, Suzanne occasionally checked her watch while casually turning the pages of a fashion magazine. Someone was tardy, but no surprise. Eventually, Ashley arrived. "I am so sorry for being late. The traffic was impossible. You know how it can be." "You always keep me waiting, but it really does not matter. We are in no rush." As Ashley made herself comfortable, a gold brooch on Suzanne's brown sleeveless blouse caught her eye. "I like your horse pin. When, where did you get it?"

Touching it fondly, she said, "Raymond gave it to me. He drove to Tiffany's in the city to find it. The purpose was to celebrate and be a remembrance of the colt's purchase." "How lovely," noted Ashley. The compliment was expanded. "Everything about Raymond is lovely. He isn't anyone. He is someone special," asserted Suzanne Wanting more detailed info, the cousin placed her hand out as though it were a stop sign. "Hey, back up a second. What about Paul? You haven't seen him for a while after the problem night. Is he really totally out of the picture?"

"Gone, my dear cousin." That tested Ashley. "Why? Don't be foolish? He is some catch." "You saw and we talked a lot about what happened at the charity ball. Have you forgotten? Macho, macho, and some more macho. The only person Paul could ever love . . . is Paul." Her luncheon companion tried again. "You two seemed happy together and being with a celebrity should be exciting." The chairman's daughter was ready to tell all. "Paul has looks, his muscles have muscles, and he could be overwhelmingly charming if he wanted. Whenever we went out for dinner, the restaurant's staff bent over backward to please us.

As people passed our table, they would smile, give us compliments, or congratulate him on the last game. Some were even forward enough and asked for his autograph. It was annoying. Maybe I was jealous, felt ignored." The storyteller hesitated, but Ashley prompted her to continue, and she willingly obliged. "Alright. What woman wouldn't be impressed with that environment? It was all superficial. The time comes when a lady must take a real look at life, deciding what she wants, what is meaningful, not what is flashy."

"Amen to that. Well then, is it really that serious with Raymond? Come on, tell me." "We share the same strong feeling about one another. Call it chemistry or whatever, it is there!" "This is so fantastic. You are in love." Wide-eyed, Ashley asked, "How is he in the bedroom?"

"Tender, sweet talks, and has a fantastic imagination. No part of the love nest is off-limits."

"Where is your favorite place?" "In the shower, being embraced with warm water splashing all over our bodies is fantastic. A woman couldn't want more. The speaker started to laugh. "It is so funny when the soap slips onto the shower floor. A lot of butt bumping goes on as we try to grab the bar. Since we are not living together, the memories of a romantic evening need to last."

"Wow! I'm getting excited . . . Back to reality fast Are your parents alright with this budding romance?"

"My mother is fine with it. She trusts my judgment, but not my father. Dad is impossible. He wants me to marry a billionaire socialite." Ashley smiled, "If there were two of those around, I would take the man you do not want."

"You can have both. Words cannot describe how I feel about Raymond. I don't want anyone else." The ladies took a breather and indulged in a sip of water. Ashley withdrew a compact mirror, quickly checked her makeup, and then replaced it into her purse. "I envy you. Have you talked about anything serious with Raymond, like setting a date?"

"Not in so many words, but I feel we will, sooner than later, but there isn't any rush. I want to avoid having an all-out fight with Dad for as long as possible. Perhaps, he will soften up later."

After a pensive moment, Ashley declared, "You will both have a long bridge to cross." Suzanne was ready to elaborate on that thought, but the waiter reached the table. "Are you ladies ready to order?" Both women said yes, sitting back for a minute to decide on their choices. Up to then, their conversation on Suzanne's love life had kept them from looking at the menu and making selections. When finished with their order, Suzanne eagerly returned to the topic. "About your bridge to cross comment, you are so right about a bridge to cross, but here is how I see it . . . Raymond is a dedicated person by nature, and money is not god for him. In his own way, he found out with politeness my position on wealth and was satisfied with the answer. A problem solved."

Ashley clapped her hands. "At least you are both on the same bridge regarding money, going the same way. Keep going. Tell me more." "We both also have a strong attraction to Thoroughbreds, and he is a good trainer. So that aspect of togetherness is perfect. I see him as a caring, honest man who loves me and says what he believes. Raymond is deeply involved in life. How are those qualities for a start?" "Some fellows never have those traits. Suzanne, this guy is perfect for you."

"Yet with those characteristics, the most important one is yet to be told. When he touches me or holds me, my whole- body warms. Only love can explain that feeling. I would go anyplace in the world to stay with him."

"Cousin, you are hooked." Ashley then put the last piece of the puzzle on the table. "What then about your father. How long can you wait for him to see it . . . your way?" "Don't have an answer to that question, and Raymond would have to be part of it. He is patient and understanding but for how long? We must get passed Dad, the toll booth collector on the bridge. Dad will try to stop us in any way that will work. It is impossible for him to get past the prestige of belonging to high society, wealth, connections, Ivy League school camaraderie, and you can add on anything I have missed."

"That is enough of a list. Do you have any thoughts on moving forward?"

"My best hope from avoiding an all-out battle is Mother. She likes Raymond and knows that love is not measured by economic or social standards. Mom trusts my judgment and will be on my side as much as she can, but Dad is Dad!" An understanding Ashley added, "This toll booth collector on your long bridge is going to tie up traffic." "Dad will be stubborn, and who can tell what else will come into play? In life, the unexpected can be the most difficult of all. The destruction button is always present." She crossed her fingers. "Somehow this will work out. I believe in fate . . . I love Raymond!"

Lunch arrived and briefly became the center of attention; however, in no time, new topics were discussed. These first cousins never spoke with any time or subject-matter restrictions. It might be said that they were vocally uninhibited when together.

CHAPTER 18
A New Jockey

It was a dark Tuesday, no races that day. Inside the driveway of Juan's house sat four cars, one of them a dark blue Mercedes convertible, which was a new addition to the usual lineup of jockeys' cars. Inside were Juan, Carlos, Jose, and the invited fourth jockey shooting pool. Juan spoke to the new arrival of their jockey colony. "Alfredo, you just two weeks here from Argentina and doing great." Trying to downplay the praise, he said, "I got a top agent, and we both work, how do you say . . . hard. That's all it takes."

Expanding on that answer, Carlos added, "Come on. It takes even more than that. How many years you leading rider in your country?" "The last four years." The exact answer he wanted. "You are great rider. Everybody knows that." Alfredo winked. "Sometimes, yes, sometimes, no." The real point for this meeting was a lot more than a pool game with Carlos bringing the topic to the forefront. "We win a lot of races like you, but we know who is going . . . to win . . . and when! It makes life easier."

Concentrating on his shot, Alfredo tried to ignore that comment without being offensive. The offer was made explicitly clear again by Juan. "Join us. Make more money. It's all cash, no taxes to pay and it attracts women." Alfredo stopped playing and gave his full attention to the other jockeys. "I try to win every race I ride; have never needed any help. I don't pull horses or fix races. There isn't any other way for me to ride!"

Another feeble attempt came from Juan. "Amigo, you sure?" The Argentinian had reached the end of this invitational road. "Yes, and I think it is time for me to leave. There are some things at home to take

112

care of. Thanks for the pool game." The three jocks felt frustration from this rejection as Alfredo turned his back on them and left the room. Dejectedly, Juan allowed himself to flop down onto a couch. "You can bet Sonny ain't gonna like this. Alfredo is a top rider. He must be one of us . . . We need him. Why is he so damn stubborn?" This thought was backed up by Carlos. "We offered him a good deal to be in with us, and in so many nice words, he told us to go fuck ourselves! He shoulda stayed in Argentina." The answer to the problem came from Juan, "Tell Sonny. He'll figure it out. This is as much his problem as ours." The three jockeys continued to play pool.

Shortly thereafter, the front door was abruptly opened, and Sonny came rushing in. This grand entrance was to intimidate the new rider. Whoever this person was, whatever his status, he should be aware of who was the boss. As he reached the table, Sonny picked up a pool stick, holding it out to see if it was straight. "Straight like me." The hood laughed and roughly rolled the stick onto the table, hitting some of the pool balls that were in play. The jocks tried to make a joke of it, forcing a laugh.

Acting time concluded, Sonny became serious. "Where is the new jock you want me to meet?" Unhappily, Juan told what had transpired, "Some bad news. Alfredo doesn't want to be part of us. He got the out of here fast." An air of indifference came over Sonny. "Too bad for him. Tell me something about this jerk." Alfredo's lifestyle spilled out from Carlos's mouth: "Every morning he goes to Prospect Park at 5:00 a.m. to jog then drives to the track and works horses for his clients. You know where he is in the afternoon . . .beating us! He has already won two races for Masterson, who you hate, and that trainer belonged to us for a long time. Those two are starting to get chummy, and it won't take Alfredo long to make solid contacts with other trainers. Not good for us."

A final touch was added by Juan, "At night, after the races, he stays home with his wife and kids. He doesn't have much of a life." "That's more than I need to know. This son of a bitch won't be a problem for long." The jockeys were puzzled by the certainty and quickness of his response. How could any situation be solved with a pledge of immediate termination from such a limited discussion? They thought they better not ask too many questions because they were afraid of the answers.

It was 5:10 a.m., four days after the jockeys had played pool. Alfredo's Mercedes drove into a parking area of Prospect Park. This 586 acres of parkland located on Flatbush Avenue, Brooklyn, had eateries, a zoo, botanical gardens, and playgrounds including a classic merry-go-round. There was also a serene lake, sixty acres in size, including several islands, with rental rowboats available to reach them. In wooded arears were facilities for picnicking and nearby were bicycle and jogging trails. At this early hour in the morning, only a few other cars were scattered throughout the large parking lot. Most runners hadn't yet tied on their running shoes.

Alfredo, who was wearing a blue jogging suit, put on headphones, allowing him to be at peace with the world. It was a perfect morning to jog; the temperature was in the low seventies while a mild breeze awakened the scents from the surrounding woodland. The only apparent activity was from several squirrels darting across his path. As he disappeared into one of the multiple private trails available no one else was around, however: two young men, also in jogging clothes, exited from their station wagon, following him.

The jockey ran at a steady pace, enjoying the music, completely unaware of being followed. The pursuers continually closed the gap between them and their prey. One finally passing the target on his right side; the other trailed behind. The appearance of another person surprised the jogger, but he had no reason to fear danger. After the first hitman went several feet past Alfredo, he turned around abruptly, causing the jockey to crash broadside into him.

Naturally, to keep from falling, both grabbed each other, allowing the killer to easily stab his victim repeatedly. The second killer ran up from behind, using a butcher's knife to slash the jockey several times along the back and side of his neck. Alfredo's jugular vein was severed, they wanted to be sure there wasn't any chance of survival. In no time, the jockey's eyes rolled; blood squirted from his mouth as he quivered to the ground.

The hitmen stared at him then rapidly ran off. The squirrels were the only witnesses to the killing. The contract had been executed! They could drive home, take a quick shower, wash off the blood, enjoy breakfast, and then go back to sleep! How many people can start work at 5:10 a.m. and be done by 5:15 a.m.?

Two hours later, Lily's patrons who were having their usual morning coffee break, talked about the previous day's races, or any recent racing scandals. An excited owner rushed in. "Did you hear?" He caught his breath. "Are you aware of what just happened?" Several asked the same question at the same time, "Hear what? What are you yelling about?" "They found Alfredo Silva killed at Prospect Park. He was knifed to death!"

One trainer in the restaurant didn't believe what he was hearing. "Murdered? Are you sure?" "It's on the radio. Is that sure enough?" Another trainer, who was finding the truth hard to understand, asked, "Who would want to kill him? The poor guy just got here. Nobody even knew him." The eating establishment became completely silent. Everyone was stunned; all were at loss to offer any words or thoughts at that moment. Even though Alfredo was there for only a short period of time, he was one of them, a respected horseman with a bright future in New York.

The atmosphere in a pub that night was quite different. Happily eating and drinking, Bruno and Sonny were found in a known gangland hangout in Gerritsen Beach, Brooklyn. Most of the patrons were regulars as the proprietor arranged it to be that way. New patrons were treated with indifference, so they gave up and never came back, thereby giving this place little new business. What John Sabatini, alias Johnny Sparks, really wanted to do was to place a neon sign, four feet high by six feet wide, in the main window which flashed, "Gangsters Only."

Everyone who passed Bruno acknowledged him, with several ladies giving him hugs and kisses. He glowed at the attention as if he were a king holding court. Other hood soldiers came to that table and had short but serious talks with him, during which time, envelopes filled with cash were often passed under the table while orders on what to do next were whispered above the table.

Glowing attention seemed to evade Sonny; he seemed lost. It appeared that he was slightly inebriated, and this displeased Bruno. "You're drinking too much. Don't get drunk on me. Pay attention to what's going on."

Raising his shoulders, Sonny defended himself, "Was the job I had done this morning sober enough for you?" The complainer backed off; "Yeah, yeah. You done what was needed . . . Perfect."

As an explanation of his condition, he said, "I'm not a drunk. If anything has me drinking more, it's that Masterson prick. This guy has got to go. He has been around too long . . . What I did to his horses that night at the barn don't come close enough to destroying him! Let me make this snitch disappear!" Pensively, Bruno said, "Yeah. The question is how? What do we do . . . drop him off the Brooklyn Bridge in a gunny sack?"

The muscle enforcer perked up. "Why not? It's a great idea?" It was time to remind Sonny of what he had already been told. "Vito musta had a sit-down with Tommy Z, and we come out the big losers. We can't touch Raymond. Uncle Vito is watching his ass, and fucking with Vito Di Mario is asking for it! Those who did"—and he rapidly threw his arms up into the air, "Gone that fast, like forever!"

The leader, completely holding Sonny's full attention went on, "When we take care of this problem, we must show our fucking strength our way, in a different way and avoid Vito's wrath. The message to anybody is, 'Mess with us, and you're finished!' Vito can't stop that. Tommy never said that we couldn't do nothing. We already have, and I intend to finish it!"

There was a different twist for Sonny; he pointed out the recent success, "Like this morning's message. Our jocks are scared shitless of us. If I say jump, they will jump before I tell them how high." The main man laughed, then he rubbed Sonny on the back before they engaged in a spontaneous high five: "Now, that's what I'm fucking talking about. This thing with Masterson is a long way from over, bet your ass on that."

Lifting his head up and down, Sonny used that motion as a gesture to acknowledge that he was being recognized for getting rid of Alfredo and other praises long overdue. As a salute to himself, he slowly drew a bent cigarette from an almost empty, crushed pack in his shirt pocket, and with an unsteady hand, he lighted a match.

Bruno became fixated on the flame that danced tauntingly before his eyes! His thoughts took him somewhere else; it was as if he wasn't physically present any longer in the bar.

CHAPTER 19
A Sure Thing Races Again

Placing the saddle on # three, "A Sure Thing," for his second outing brought a new challenge. This day of races never saw the sun; there were constant heavy showers, which caused the racing surface to have an abundance of water on it, causing it to be labeled sloppy.

The trainer commented, "Another test today." Sensing anxiety, Suzanne asked, "Raymond are you nervous?" "An off track always gives me concern. Some horses can't handle it. You never know until they try." The lady gave encouragement for it was proper for a lady to do so. "He will be alright. Don't worry." Full of energy, her colt confidently pranced around the paddock. Finally, as the jockey was given a leg up, Raymond reluctantly gave some last-minute instructions, "Steve, try to go to the front and get away from getting hit by a ton of mud."

The jockey laid out a foolproof plan to execute that request, "Sure, Ray that's easy. Just tell the other jocks to let me do it." Laughing, the trainer gave Steve a pat on his boot. He and Suzanne then left the paddock area to sit in their usual spot. After arriving there, both had their binoculars at the ready.

Announcer: "Last to load, No. seven, "Fire Chief" and they're off . . . "A Sure Thing" again shoots to the lead, but he has company. "Real Motion" is at his side." After one-quarter mile into the race, Raymond points to the fractions on the tote board. "Way too fast. A quarter in twenty-two seconds flat is flying!" Another possibility was suggested by the lady, "Maybe the track surface is hard even though it has water on it." Announcer: "A speed dual upfront. The half-mile in forty-five. "Power" in third; "Tandem," fourth; "Circle Us" is fifth;" Of Course," sixth; "Fire Chief" last."

Little changed in positions until they hit the top of the stretch. Announcer: "Real Motion" is tiring. "Power" moves into second place, "Tandem," third, "Circle Us," a distant fourth. A Sure Thing" still in command. He's picking them up and putting them down." This pleased Raymond. "He likes the mud. His action is smooth." Announcer: "As they hit the finish line, "A Sure Thing" wins under no pressure by six lengths; "Power" second; "Tandem," third; "Circle Us," fourth."

"Maybe he likes everything." It was Suzanne's hope. In tandem with her judgment, he said, "You won't hear any different from me. Nothing seems to bother this colt, yet." Announcer: "Easy winner again . . . "A Sure Thing" . . . time, a respectable seven-eights- of a mile in 1 minute twenty-two seconds."

"Are you thinking what I am thinking?" Asked the owner in anticipation. "Yes. I believe so. This is probably a stake horse. Your colt deserves a shot in the upcoming stake race . . . It's two weeks away from this Saturday. The timing is perfect . . . What a horse you bought!" There was a polite correction, "No, dear, we bought it . . . Remember? We were together."

The following morning, during a training break, they decided to enjoy their favorite breakfast place. It was crowded, making it necessary for them to sit at the counter, which was not as comfortable or semiprivate as a table. As people passed, they congratulated the winners on their recent victory. The racing colony was always aware of the previous day's races, thereby making compliments normal conversation, even expected.

Beautiful Suzanne was basking in the victory and congratulations but sought reassurance from her lover about the future. "Do you still want to run in that stake race? A three-hundred-thousand-dollar purse at a mile distance. It won't be easy. Is he ready? Maybe we are moving him along too quickly?" Having no doubts in his confidence and the horse Raymond was unwavering. "I believe so. His training for me is right on schedule, even better." "I knew that is what you would say, but I needed to hear it."

"Here is a wild thought," said Raymond. "Win that race, and you own the favorite for next year's Kentucky Derby." The owner became wide-eyed. "Who could have ever thought we would be this fortunate?" A request from Raymond, "Keep your fingers crossed. Stay a lucky lady."

The track was crowded the day of the stake race as it usually was on Saturday afternoon. Excitement filled the air; bettors were motivated by a good racing card under ideal weather conditions. People were at the windows, betting; small groups gathered to talk, handicap, laugh, eat, and down a beer or two or three or more. In the jockeys' room, Juan and Carlos sat on a wooden bench close to each other, out of hearing range of the other jockeys. Juan nervously slid over even closer to Carlos. This plot fell under the category of top secret. "We must make "A Sure Thing" lose." It was Juan's concern.

"Have a little trust, Juan. No sweat. We bump him a couple of times, block him, and he will be out of the race . . . We do that kind of stuff all the time. His jockey won't know what hit him. Kelly and Masterson don't know we are doing business with Sonny and that he told us what to do. They don't suspect nothing."

This plan worried Juan and for good reason. "There can't be any screwups! Sonny don't want this horse to win. He's acting loco, and we don't want to get him any crazier than he already is. I'm afraid of him." Settling Juan's nerves was Carlos's main objective. "You could do this in your sleep. Don't waste time thinking about the race. It is better that way." Race time was approaching. In the paddock with their jockey. Raymond and Suzanne waited patiently for the call, "Riders up/"

Upon passing Raymond, Juan waved his whip, speaking to him as if nothing was going down, "Good luck, compadre." The thoughtful gesture was returned, "And to you. A safe trip." Raymond had no possible conception of the devious plan that was organized to defeat his jockey. The "Good luck, compadre" greeting from Juan was an outright lie to cover up his devious plan. Evil minds work overtime to be deceitful.

Raymond had not yet put a connection between Bruno, Sonny, and the jockeys. To him, the gangsters were into drugging horses, and that was where the story ended. The paddock judge called, "Riders up!" The jocks were given a leg up, pointing their Thoroughbreds in the direction of the racetrack. As "A Sure Thing" started smartly to move away from

Raymond, he spoke hurriedly to his rider, "Steve, give me your extra best. This race means a lot . . ."

"You always get that from me. I ride like I own them." The black saddle towel with the number six sat firmly against "A Sure Thing's" gleaming chestnut body. His name was boldly printed in gold letters directly under the number. Suzanne's colt was in a field with ten, and as the horses warmed up. Kelly noticed that Juan and Carlos had left their pony boys. They had separated themselves from the others and were in constant conversation. This was not part of a normal post-parade warmup.

Steve speaking to the pony boy at his side, asked, "What are those two thieves drumming up?" "Whatever it is, it ain't no good for somebody." "Yeah," echoed Steve. "And I'm getting that somebody feeling." Kelly and his pony rider continued to stare at Juan and Carlos, but the two were oblivious to the world.

All the horses continued to the starting place and were loaded in numerical order into that solid iron structure, the starting gate. In the field, # seven, "Cosmic Change," was ridden by Juan, and Carlos rode # 3 three, "Bit of Luck." Announcer: "It is now post time for the featured race of this afternoon, the ¾-million-dollar, 1-mile Gallantly Forward Stakes. They're set in the starting gate. Hold on . . . Number five, "Joe's Place," is acting up . . . He's steadied . . . and . . . their off!" Immediately, when the gate sprung open, Juan on "Cosmic Change," cut "A Sure Thing," off badly! Steve had to sharply check his mount or fall as his colt stumbled!

It demanded all the jockey's skills and strength to regain his own balance and stay in the stirrups while keeping his mount from going down! This acrobatic move caused the horse and rider to immediately drop back to the last place. Moving the binoculars from his eyes, the trainer commiserated with Suzanne, "What just happened? He is last! I don't believe it."

"He has always broken so well. I don't know," was the lady's comment. Announcer: "A Sure Thing" breaks poorly, trials the field!" The couple, along with the crowd on hand, was puzzled. Announcer: "Cosmic Change" in front, "Best of Luck" second, followed by "Hard Spot" with "Mystic Man" alongside. But still trailing is "A Sure Thing."

"He is in trouble" was all that the lady could sadly say.

"Not the right day for trouble. It is about impossible to overcome that terrible start," was Raymond's take. Announcer: "They go down the backstretch with little change in positions . . . They are reaching the half-mile-mile pole, in a modest forty-seven seconds. "Cosmic Change" still with a comfortable lead." The trainer projected, "We need something to go right. Maybe he can save ground on the turn, get through on the rail." Announcer: "They are reaching the top of the stretch. "Cosmic Change" has had it his own way, with no pressure on the front. "A Sure Thing" is starting to make a bold bid, going wide to get a running room lane."

The owner became a realist. "So much for saving ground. Our horse is not going to win this race. We have no chance. Announcer: "The favorite has a lot of work to do." As Steve moved, he saw Carlos directly in front of him, turning his head, searching his right side then his left side. As Steve started to drift out for a clear running path, so did Carlos, to make certain that his target lost even more ground. Steve gambled and brazenly ducked inside of Carlos. The sudden move worked. "A Sure Thing" was clear, and Carlo's devious part of the plan to interfere had backfired. Carlos mumbled to himself, "Mierda! Oh, mierda!" Announcer: The favorite finds a place to run and is charging hard.

He is gaining, gaining with each powerful stride, but the finish line is coming up fast." Suzanne and Raymond, lost in time, were holding their breath. Win or lose, this type of a stretch duel was not the way they imagined the finish to unfold. Announcer: "Each horse is all out. Look at this, racing fans. Jockey Kelly is not using his whip! He knows that his mount is already giving his everything!"

On the other hand, it was evident to all race watchers that Juan was pounding away with his stinging whip on the abused "Cosmic Change" right shoulder where multiple welt marks were evident. This poor horse was running his heart out to escape terror! Announcer: "They're at the finish line. It's a nose, a nose or less either way. What a horse race! Hold all pari-mutuel tickets until this fantastic finish is official." The announcer had set the stage for a period of wrenching uncertainty! Everyone held an opinion, but no one was positive of the official results.

If the horses had been side by side at the finish line, an educated guess would have had value, but that was not the case here. They were widely separated from each other. "Cosmic Change" was close on the rail, and "A Sure Thing" was nearer the middle of the track, which greatly increased the difficultly in judging a tight nose or less photo. The couple were on their feet, praying, begging, hoping for victory as the horses crossed the finish line. They now concentrated on the tote board for the answer. At this moment, for them, their only entity in the world was that tote board.

Suzanne tried to rationalize the tense situation, "It does not matter to me if he won or not. He gave his absolute best. A game effort!" In short order the numbers were placed on the tote board:

7 Cosmic Change

6 A Sure Thing

2 Mystic Man

3 Bit of Luck

Raymond faced reality. "Tough beat. We had the best horse but the worst luck. There are days like that." At that moment, the numbers of the first two horses started to flash. Announcer: "There is a steward's inquiry and the jockey's objection into the start of this race against the winner. Hold all pari-mutuel tickets until the result is declared official."

When numbers flashed on the tote board at a racetrack, the patrons became silent. An inquiry could take one minute or five minutes or more, but however long, it always seemed like an eternity. If there is a disqualification, there will be two roars from the crowd. The first, when a disqualified number was taken down, and the second, when the winning number had been posted in the proper place. If the result remains the same, with no change, the patrons will holler only once.

The lady tried to be optimistic. "Still hope." But she revealed deeper feelings when she said, "I'll never survive this ordeal." Pushing himself to think outside of the inquiry, Raymond said, "Let's go check on our horse and speak to the rider."

When they reached their destination, their jockey, who had just been talking on the phone with the stewards joined them. "I claimed a foul against the winner. I almost got killed at the start, and Carlos tried to make it impossible to pass him in the stretch. They had something cooking." The owner had sensed that something was wrong. "We were not able to see the break clearly, but I was shocked!" The jockey interjected, "The stewards couldn't miss that infraction."

He then coldly looked over in the direction of Juan, who deliberately turned the other way as he stared at the ground. Carlos had already dismounted and was on his way back to the jockey's room. The rider leaned nearer to Raymond and confided, "I'm going to have a little talk with Juan after this is over, and one of us won't be riding for a couple of days." Understanding that mindset, the trainer encouraged, "A man has to do what he has to do!"

Out of hearing range and not wanting to miss anything, the lady asked, "What did our jockey say? I did not hear him. What did he say?" It was not possible to repeat that exact statement. A socialite might not agree with it, so Raymond had to make something up fast. "Steve said there should never be a reason for an inquiry and that he was going to do his best to make race riding safer." "How admirable. He is such a professional. Every jockey should be like him."

Her lover restrained any expression. Several minutes passed before the tote board was ready to reveal the verdict. "This is nerve-racking" was repeated twice by her. Finally, the numbers were reversed on the tote board, and it lighted up, "Official." The crowd gave the two roars. Suzanne placed her hands, over her beautiful face to cover the tears of joy.

Announcer: "The order of finish has been reversed. Number six, "A Sure Thing" has been placed first; and number seven, "Cosmic Change," has been disqualified into second place for causing interference at the start."

The official tote board reads as follows:

	Win	Place	Show
A Sure Thing 6	3.80	3.00	2.40
Cosmic Change 7		4.00	2.50
Mystic Man 2			2.80
Exacta 6---7 pays 16.40			

The Brockhurst family waited in the box for the result so to avoid the embarrassment of waiting in the winner's circle and then be required to leave if there wasn't a change in the order. Now, that a picture was ready to be snapped Charles, Isabel, and Ashley all quickly left the second-level box to join those already in the winner's circle. Hugs were in order and exchanged. However, the best Charles managed to give Raymond was a meaningless, one-time, mechanical handshake which bordered on an insult.

Reporters looking for an interview and close congratulatory friends started to surround the perimeter of the winner's circle. Isolated in their clubhouse box, Bruno and Sonny were fit to be tied. Sonny was beside himself. "Can you believe this fucking shit?" The boss had a bold answer, "Not any longer. The final payment is due! You can believe that!"

A week later, Raymond was in his office, aimlessly shuffling through conditions books and taking spare time to admire the winning picture taken of the stake race. He picked it up from the desktop several times, studied it, and then returned the photo to the original spot. Each viewing was better than the last. He, Suzanne, and "A Sure Thing" looked like movie stars.

A race tracker, employed by him unexpectedly walked into Raymond's office and caught the trainer admiring the photo. "Boss, what are ya looking at? Can I see it?" The picture was turned to be in the line of vision for Jerry, the night watchman, to see it. "Oh yeah, a picture of the stake win." That comment was expanded. "A day I will never forget," recalled the trainer. "Yeah, great. I was there. Bet a few bucks on him." The warmup time was over; there now had to be a reason for this unexpected visit. Did Jerry need a loan? "Jerry, what's up?"

Jerry always showed a slight nervous twitch on his face when hustling for something extra. "Can't night watchman tonight, but I can get ya somebody else if ya want?" For a moment, Raymond paused, gave the request some thought. "No. one night shouldn't be a problem. Who would know you're not here?" "Fuck, nobody. Thanks for the pass. Be back tomorrow night."

CHAPTER 20
A Long Night

*I*t was early that same evening, as Raymond left his apartment and went directly to his car. Tightly tucked under his right arm was a thick, four and- a-half-feet-long cardboard container. Upon reaching his Mustang, the trainer carefully placed it in the trunk. Driving directly to the track, he passed his barn # ten and found a secluded area three barns away to park. Deliberately, with care, he lifted the carton out of the trunk and brought it to the barn.

Upon entering, his first task was to check the horses and see that they were all okay. In short order it was time to settle into his office, placing the box on the desk while shutting off a desk lamp to achieve absolute darkness. Waiting, he tried to get comfortable, but that was not possible. A chair is not a bed. The clock on the wall showed 9:30 p.m.; the long hours passed unhurriedly until early morning was reached. Continued twisting and turning had caused muscle pain, and by that time, drowsiness was setting in. A silver-gray Chevy station wagon with tinted windows pulled up to the track security gate. The guard gave a quick glance to the owner's sticker on the windshield as the driver rolled down his window and showed a counterfeit owner's badge with his picture on it. The face on that plastic card was one of Alfredo Silva's killers!

The security man gave a smile and a comment, "Don't see too many owners at the barns this late." The driver volunteered a rehearsed response, "Couldn't sleep. Looking at my horse will help me relax." The guard waved him through. When the vehicle stopped at the far end of barn # ten, the back cargo door opened, and two figures emerged from the darkness inside the vehicle into the darkness of the night.

126

Finally, Raymond was rewarded. The trainer heard the sound he has been waiting for all those restless hours, which was the large, noisey barn door sliding open. The trainer stayed motionless until muffled voices were detected, then steadily, slowly got up, stretched, before touching the large box on the table. Attempting to open it, the cardboard top became stuck, and after several serious attempts, there wasn't any progress. At last, he pushed the box firmly against his body and pressed down hard on the edge. Finally, the box reluctantly popped open and revealed its cargo, a 20-gauge shotgun!

Raymond felt it, then made the sign of the cross, asking the One above for his protection. He placed the weapon in his hands while disengaging the safety catch on top. It already had a shell in the chamber and five in the magazine. Ready for war, Raymond composed himself as much as possible, then left the office! Having made their way several yards into the shed row, Bruno and Sonny were liberally pouring a clear, strongly scented liquid on the barn walls. Preoccupied with their devious endeavor, they had no awareness of the trainer's presence, nor had any reason to expect anyone else. The night watchman was gone; as arranged.

Being the first to empty his two containers, Bruno dropped them carelessly over the ground behind him and pulled out a pack of matches. It was flame time when Raymond demanded attention, "Drop the matches!" Bruno and Sonny were stunned. Raymond reached within less than six yards from them, and they never saw or heard him. "Drop the matches! No time for games! It's over!"

Obeying, Sonny started to throw them away, but as that hand reached his midsection, with a lightning strike, he grabbed into his jacket. A magician did not have quicker hands, the handle of a pistol immediately appeared. The hoodlum gambled that he would be faster on the trigger pull than this spineless trainer who probably wouldn't have the guts to shoot. Bad bet! There was a choice to make, but Raymond never thought about it that way. This was survival, payback time.

Not hesitating, Raymond fired. Bam! The shot hit Sonny squarely in the right shoulder! Flesh, bone, blood, and clothing splattered into the still night air! The pistol Sonny was drawing flew into the air and tumbled to the ground. The wounded gangster turned sideways, screamed, grabbed his torn shoulder area, and fell to the dirt, face down in agony, assuming a fetal position. At this point, after the buckshot was fired, the horses in the barn went wild, leaving it unsafe for anybody to be in a stall with them. The driver waiting outside was spooked as the horse were. What did the sound of a gunshot signal? Should he stay where he was ordered for a quick getaway or make a move to go inside? Either choice could turn out badly! He stayed where he was.

Quickly, Raymond pumped another shell into the chamber. He then gave Bruno his full attention. "Bruno don't move! Hands high! Let me see your hands!" Shaking, Bruno raised his hands as high as he was able, causing a corner of the dark brown shirt that he was wearing to come partially out of his pants. Pleading, he said, "It was his idea, honest. Let me go. I'll give you whatever you want . . . How much?" "Forget it, Bruno. Your money is dirty. Give me half a reason, and you join your friend on the ground."

The arsonist continued to tremble. Right then eyeball to eyeball, less than six feet away, Raymond stared at Bruno. They were locked together in a drama, no words were needed. A shotgun at that distance displayed potentially awesome firepower, comparable to a cannon, and Bruno was on the wrong side of it.

The gangster's uncontrolled passion to destroy Raymond and to personally deliver the blow could have been in a literary work worthy of Shakespeare. This was the final, spectacular scene where the principal character's sins destroyed him. Bruno had a hard time keeping his arms elevated, one of which had splashes of Sonny's blood on it. When his arms started to drop, Raymond warned him again, "Hands high!" The trainer wasn't taking any chances.

Stopping, he glanced at a fire alarm box on the wall. Smashing the glass with the butt of the shotgun, the handle was pulled. "This should get us company fast" The strong alarm siren wailed. In the racetrack security office, there were four men. One desk sign read, "Lt. Mario Marigone," while the other three desks were without names. Most of the time, one or two of those men would be on patrol in their vehicles.

Lieutenant Mario blurted out, "What going on here? A gunshot . . . a fire alarm!" Glancing to his assistants he gave a straight order, "Call both the firehouse and the ambulance together. We are confirming that it's barn # ten, but if they arrive first, tell them don't dare to go in . . . until we get there. Something strange is happening. This is a dangerous situation." The four men rush out into two security vehicles and, with full speed, raced to barn ten. One truck went to the front of the barn, and the other to the back.

The security vehicles arrived first before the ambulance or firetruck. Lieutenant Marigone and his partner found the gray station wagon with its engine running and, immediately, with guns drawn, opened their doors at the same time as did Bruno's man. He exited with a gun in one hand, throwing up his left arm to shield his eyes from the headlights and spotlights of the security truck. The lieutenant screamed, "Drop your weapon. You don't have a chance!"

Both security men were ready to pull the triggers. The gangster, half-blinded from the headlights, wasn't even certain how many weapons were pointed at him! Throwing his weapon to the ground in front of him, his arms reached high into the air. After a body search that revealed an eight -inch butcher knife; he was placed in handcuffs. Keeping that captive in front of them and manipulating him by his cuffed wrists, they carefully stepped into the barn, not knowing what to expect.

Entering the barn, the security team had their pistols at the ready! In front of the security force, Sonny lay on the ground, and Bruno was held at bay. The lieutenant, who knew Raymond, yelled out. "Ray, what's going on?"

Excitedly, the trainer answered, "These two gangsters were going to burn down my barn, killing me and all my horses, but I got them first!" The retired New York City police detective and his assistants, all four, were now together. Meanwhile, the ambulance and firetruck, several minutes behind the security team, pulled up outside, arriving at the same time. Since the paramedics saw a twisted body on the ground, they instinctively rushed over to Sonny. Their evaluation was prompt. "This guy needs the hospital right away! He's losing a lot of blood."

The lieutenant agreed. "Take care of him." Attending to Sonny as best as they were able, the paramedics placed him on a stretcher and were ready to remove him from the barn. There was a last-minute directive from the lieutenant. "We can't wait for the police to arrive. I don't want this guy to die here. I'll notify their office of the circumstances and have the police meet you at the hospital. One of my armed security guards will join you and keep an eye on the wounded man."

The two medics nodded in understanding and accepted the lieutenant's order and his insight. It was time for Marigone to question the trainer, "Raymond, do you know who he is?"

"Yes, his handle is Sonny, associated with a horse owner who had a couple of horse with me." Distracted for a moment by the shotgun in Raymond's hands, he said, "Hey, that artillery can be put away." The shotgun was placed against the wall.

Quickly the lieutenant gave the gangster a professional pat down. Reaching Bruno's side, he stopped, "What is this?" Pulling a Smith & Wesson forty caliber semiautomatic pistol from Bruno's black holster, he declared, "You won't have to use this anytime soon. Probably never!" Then giving his attention to Sonny's weapon on the ground, he took two clean towels off the window- sill and placed both pistols loosely in them. "The one you picked up from the ground belongs to Sonny. He is the gangster who drew on me, and I had to shoot him. It was my life or his!"

"Good move. I give you credit. Not an easy thing to shoot anybody. We almost had to plug one of them outside! My heart is still racing! I'll give these weapons to the police." The firemen now had brought chemical extinguishes into the barn and systematically foamed down the walls. They were scrupulous to detail. Speaking with his two remaining assistants about the prisoners, the lieutenant said, "Put cuffs on this other bird too. Bring both to our office. We will turn the prisoners over to the police. Don't take your eyes off them."

And in a loud, bellowing voice so that there wasn't any chance for the gangsters not to hear it, he said, "Keep your weapons drawn and use them, if you have to!" The security officers escorted the pair out of the barn. With three firemen at his side, the fire chief then gave Lieutenant

Marigone his findings, "The stuff they used was highly flammable, and this barn would have been burnt toast in no time. However, there is no longer a threat. We are ready to leave" Relieved to hear that final evaluation, Marigone said, "Thank you. Chief, please leave your report in my office." Picking up their equipment, they gave the area a last visual check and then departed.

There was a moment of quiet. The two looked at each other. Finally, Raymond started a conversation. "Lieutenant, Bruno and Sonny are violent people. They drugged horses and from what I have seen in races that I ran in, there is a connection between Bruno and crooked jockeys. There were strong rumors going around the backstretch that races were set up. I'm sure these crumbs were somehow involved in race fixing and probably the murder of Jockey Alfredo Silva." "These are serious charges to consider," replied the lieutenant. "However, there is something to clear up before we go any further. Are these the same rats who attacked your barn the last time you had trouble? I'll never forget that night."

"Who else could it have been? They were the only people out to harm me. That it happened once made me think that tonight might be try-again time. My night watchman took off, and I became suspicious."

"They are not going to get away with any crimes. Our track security division will work with the police to uncover all their dirty works and coconspirators at the Racetrack. We want racing to be honest." "That's encouraging. Those two had no sense of right or wrong, only getting what they wanted, no matter what got destroyed or who got hurt."

Scratching his head, Marigone expressed his state of mind, "What a night this has been. A shooting, an attempted arson, murder suspects arrested. I'm back on the police force. What's left to do?" Throwing his fists straight up into the air Raymond shouted: "I hope nothing . . . double nothing!"

"You better stick around. The police will want to speak with you" was the lieutenant's last piece of advice. Raymond glanced at his Hamilton watch. "All right. Anyway, it's almost time to start work. I'll catch a little sleep in my office and wait for the police."

CHAPTER 21
The Police Arrived

At his desk, eyes shut and dozing off, Raymond heard a sharp knock on the door, which aroused him. The trainer shook his head to focus as he was in the middle of a sexy dream. No, it wasn't Lola. Only romantic dreams of Suzanne were allowed. The question, "Who is it?" came in a low tone. The response was clear: "Detectives Randy Pricci and Jim Brady . . . Nassau County Police Department, Fifth District. May we come in and speak with you?" The weary horseman shook his head several times, ran fingers through his hair, and said, "Come on in." Upon meeting the two detectives, it was obvious that there was a large age gap between them.

Detective Pricci appeared to be in his early thirties while Detective Brady was mid- fifties. The men were invited to sit down. "I guess Lieutenant Marigone told you what went on here." Brady confirmed, "Of course. My good old friend detective—no, excuse me . . . I should have given him the right grade he deserves . . . I mean Lieutenant Marigone gave us a full verbal and signed written report for backup, but still there are questions and procedures for us to follow. We always request the same from all witnesses. We need the whole picture in our records to submit a correct report. A shooting is always more paperwork."

The observant Detective Brady placed his attention on the shotgun at the corner of the office. "Is that the weapon you used?" "Yes, sir, it is." The same detective asked, "Out of curiosity, is it currently registered?" "Sure, sir, under my name. I have owned it since 1960 for hunting purposes."

Wanting to dilute the tension that Raymond was experiencing due to the stress of an inquiry, the young detective suggested, "Please, drop the 'sir' part when you speak with us. I'm Randy and he is Jim . . . Relax." "Thank you for understanding, but for me, the law is the law, and I respect it and you both, but your suggestion makes me comfortable. Now, you are giving me the courtesy of being my friends." The trainer smiled.

"It always makes questioning easier if you can be at ease," said Randy. "Now let's get back to the shotgun. We have to take it as evidence." "Go ahead but be careful. It is still loaded . . . Detectives, am I in any sort of trouble?" While moving his head sideways left to right, looking directly into Raymond's eyes, Detective Pricci answered, "Not at all! You had every right to protect your animals, and property from arson, and yourself from a deadly assault. You may come out of this . . . a hero." "What the heck does a hero feel like?" asked Raymond. "I'll have to read a book on the subject." "You don't have to read anything. If people say that you are a hero . . . don't argue!"

That joke brought any tension level that still existed to zero. Getting back to the task at hand, the older detective probed deeper, "Are we correct that two other men were with the wounded man?"

"Yes, a driver. I don't know him. Then there was Bruno La Scala, the leader. The action wasn't unfolding as expected, and the gangster realized that this was not the place for him to be. He was nervous. About the shooting, I didn't have a choice. Everything happened fast. It was him or me. I acted on instinct. There wasn't time for a decision to do it or not. Deep down, I didn't want a choice. It was deliverance day . . . I fired!" A revealing insight into their lives came from Detective Brady. "We know about the survival instinct feeling too well in our own way. It is part of our everyday existence.

We never know when or where it will happen, a basic uncertainty of how we live and sometimes die." Referring back to the weapons Raymond informed them that "Lieutenant Marigone has Sonny's and Bruno's pistols. Did he tell you that Bruno never had a chance or any desire to draw his gun? He saw what happened to his partner."

"Yes. We have the pistols now. Okay, what we need is that full written statement covering all the detail about which we speak." "Here is one that I wrote up in case you asked for one . . . Tried to be accurate and complete." We have our forms but will take your outline. After the investigation is finished, you will have to sign our report. How long have you known all these men?"

"One of them, the driver who was outside, I never saw him before. The others, Bruno, a year, and Sonny, whatever his real name is, for about two months. I want to forget him as soon as possible. He was brutal!"

The gap was filled in by Detective Pricci, "Sonny's real name is Gabriel DeVano, Bruno's twenty-seven-year-old cousin, born in Naples. Been in and out of jail for assault twice, but the victims were afraid and never showed up to press charges. So the law had to let him walk." "There is no walking this time. He will crawl! Remember Jockey Alfredo Silva, who was killed? I believe Bruno and Sonny were involved. They may have had control over some jockeys, and the Argentinian didn't fit the picture."

"That's interesting," replied Detective Pricci. "Lieutenant Marigone relayed your suspicion to us, and we weren't surprised to hear the connection. That murder case is very much alive. It wouldn't be too difficult to suspect that the killer was somehow involved in the racing world." Detective Brady added, "Let me assure you, the investigation of your situation and anything associated with it will be thorough." "These guys deserve the hammer of justice. They are . . . bastards! Real bastards!" was Raymond's conclusion. "They're not going to get away this time. We are going to stop them. Trust me! They are going to jail . . . no question," assured Detective Brady. "They were caught red-handed!"

Speaking of future activity regarding the case, Detective Pricci gave a rough outline: "Be prepared to hear from the prosecutor's office. You are the main witness in this case." Hearing this pleased the trainer. "I look forward to cooperating and probably can tell the prosecutors more than they may suspect, at least I hope so . . . You gentlemen are always welcomed back to the stable or perhaps join me for an afternoon at the races. Bring your families." They shook hands. Sobering parting words came from Detective Pricci, "Glad everything worked out the way it did. You were playing with fire and, somehow, got lucky. You could have been dead by now!" With the detectives gone; Raymond returned to his armchair. He didn't want to think or talk. Peace at last!

CHAPTER 22
Suzanne Finds Out

*I*t was time to train; barn activities had started, and Raymond was moving around. His crew was working, horses were being groomed, and some of them already walked in the shed row. A few minutes' break was needed, so he returned to his office, beginning to aimlessly shuffle some condition books around. Although doing normal functions, he was not ready to move at full speed; perhaps the whole day would be in slow motion.

The door opened unexpectedly, allowing an anxious Suzanne to enter quickly. Surprised, Raymond jumped up as Suzanne moved toward him, hugging and kissing her lover again and again, "Are you alright? I heard what happened last night. How horrible! Were you hurt?" "No, but one of the gangsters is in bad shape." This was a recollection time for Suzanne. "Now it all comes together, scratching La Scala's runners . . . the attack on the horses at the barn . . . the suspicion about your horses not running well, "A Sure Thing having troubles in the stake race and now this." The lady was shocked. "I can't begin to reach the misery and stress that you were experiencing!" "For starters, they forced me to run Tenor although he was drugged. When they did it to both horses the next time, I couldn't be involved in their crooked game again. It wasn't happening."

"Why did you keep it a secret from me?" "I didn't want those slimy bums anywhere near you or even have you know they existed. Getting you involved was the last thing I could ever have wanted . . . Not an option in any way." "How caring. Did you ever consider telling the stewards or the police?" "Yes, but it was a no-win situation. Bruno and Sonny were only going to deny my accusation. They threatened to say I was involved in their dirty scheme. I had no witnesses, only my word against theirs . . . The situation was only going to get worse before it got better." "You were up against it." "That you could bet on. Once the horses were scratched, I knew it was going to be rough. That type only knows one thing, how to get revenge." "I feel a closeness to you as never before" was Suzanne's confession. "Being near you, touching you gave me strength during this tough time. Suzanne, how could I have survived without you?

Wanting to hear even more from her lover, she asked, "Do you believe in fate?" "Never gave it much thought." "Well . . . I believe in fate." Cautiously, Raymond offered a possible example, "The first time I saw you, by chance, I fell in love. Sounds crazy, is that what you mean . . . by fate?" "Yes. I also felt a reaction when our eyes met, but it was so fast, so unexpected. I thought, here is a fine-looking man, and it was over. The love bug bit you hard, and you had to wait for me to catch up. That was the beginning of fate pulling us together. We did nothing to plan love." While looking at each other, a spiritual moment embraced the pair.

No more words were needed or could be found. The ecstasy was interrupted by an exercise rider swinging a pair of blinkers in his hand when he barged into the office. The rider had a question. "Do ya want—" He stopped cold in his tracks as soon as he saw them in each other's arms. Making light of it because the poor rider was unaware, Raymond said, "Not now, Marko. Let me catch up with you in a few minutes." "Sorry, boss, real sorry. Didn't see ya busy."

As soon as the rider exited the room, Raymond went over and locked the door. The top half of it had smoky glass construction and the bottom part solid metal. They joined back into each other's arms. The outlines of horses and people gracefully passing behind the frosted glass of the shut door could be seen. It gave a merry-go-round effect. "I love you so much that it hurts!" she whispered. They kissed passionately. Raymond was the first to break the intimacy. "Suzanne, I would be lost without you. The first time we spoke, I tried to hide my feelings from you, but you could tell." "It was the game of love . . . It was easy to see how you felt, quite flattering, but I was involved in a relationship at that time. It was the way it was, however, I showed you respect and was always honest with you."

Running his hand through the beautiful woman's hair, he said, "How do we stay together?" Suzanne had the perfect answer, "When a man asks his lady that question properly, she will say yes or no." Knowing what needed to be said, he was yet still cautious. "Suzanne, what about your family? Will they accept me? I'm not exactly in the social register or world famous. You shouldn't have to struggle and be hurt defending our love."

"Sweetheart don't let it be a concern. I am my own woman. Besides, the legacy that my grandmother left me is enough inheritance to buy . . . the Social Register." At that option, he paused. "Well, that's one way for me to get in, through the back door." They both laughed.

"What is status anyway? It means absolutely nothing to me. You are a loving, gentle man. What is more precious?" There was not a moment of silence before the reply was presented, "Only with you! Suzanne Brockhurst, could I have heaven on Earth?---Be my wife!" "I will!" was the clear and determined affirmation. They embraced as one, gently swaying in each other's arms as they kissed.

"Now do you understand and believe in fate? It brought us together for a purpose." "Yes, but is fate a forever thing?" "Always and forever, darling. Always and forever. Fate is a sure thing." Their sensual embrace continued as will their true love. Each shall endlessly share a part of the other!

That afternoon, Raymond became uneasy about the aftermath of the previous night's shootout, needing to talk to people in whom he could confide his uncertainties. There was no one better to speak to about the underworld than Uncle Vito, who was available to meet him that evening at the restaurant. Entering the eatery, he found his uncle sitting in the back of the dining area, the exact same spot where he had met Tommy Z. Vito didn't stand but moved a chair back for Raymond to sit. Vito always spoke his mind. "You don't look so good." "I only got about two hours sleep. Guess you know why I am here?" "You mean lucky to be here. What were you're doing, shooting it out with a hitman? Are you nuts? That was the time to call me! I would have got the right men for the job."

This rough language made Raymond realize just how much of a risk had been taken; how foolish he might have been. "I was playing a hunch, not sure myself what was going to happen, and you didn't need to be bothered again." "You did it. Let's move on. Why are you here?" "Is it over?" a worried Raymond asked. "I feel terrible about having to come back to ask you questions." "My nephew, you are never a bother. From the word around, the other guys gonna get a lot of visits from the police. Any of their boys involved in that racing scam are already underground or leaving town. Bruno and Sonny are going to be in jail for a long time, and it's their fault. Stupid is stupid! That gang will forget about you. They don't need any more trouble. I will make sure that it's understood. Go ahead. Figure it's over."

Repeatedly yawning, Raymond tried hard to justify his past actions to Vito, "I've been under a lot of pressure, trapped. Something had to snap! Don't know how much more I could have taken? I had to act!" Uncle Vito roared with laughter. "Forget it. You are more like your uncle than anybody thought. Great! Maybe the one difference is that I would have shot both dead, but that's me." Then he gave Raymond a slap on the back, officially closing the meeting with, "I'm proud of you. Enjoy a good meal, go home, get to bed, and don't ever do it again." Two days later, Raymond called his ailing mentor, Joe Hardy, making a date to visit early the next afternoon. Uncle Vito was in tune with the underworld, but Joe was the expert on day-to-day racing.

As Joe's wife ushered Raymond into the living room, it was obvious that the old-timer was paler, frailer, not looking as well as several weeks earlier. Joe's health was in rapid decline. This caused the visitor sadness for he wanted to remember the septuagenarian as a well-kept, spry, healthy gentleman. Raymond greeted his old friend, "How are things going?" Not about to give a tale of grief, Joe settled on, "As you get older, some problems slip into your life. You have to make the best of them."

"If there is ever, ever, anything that I can do, you know, call." "Sure. How are things working out for you at the track? What happened the other night?" "Some bad people tried to burn my barn, and I caught them." "I have never heard of that before." In the phone call, you said there was something to talk about. Was that it?" "No, sir. There are situations with the jockeys that don't add up. I was at a party in Greenwich Village where Jockey Jose was also a guest. He casually asked me how things were. The first thought that came to my mind was that I had run a filly earlier in the week who should have been an easy winner. She didn't."

"And?" asked Joe. Jose had the perfect answer, "You had no shot." "I let his remark slide. She ran back ten days later at a higher level of completion, winning easily. That jockey knew something about the previous race. It was fixed, and he was involved." "Well, son, crooked jocks have always been a part of the game, sometimes worse than others. A beautiful business and they can only think of stealing."

"Listen to this one. I was standing in the paddock, waiting for my rider when Carlos walked past. We greeted each other, after which, he said, "You win this race. I did. If the race wasn't fixed, how would he know that my horse would be the winner? There are other things happening at this time that can't be put on the table." "Only track security can enforce integrity. It is beyond you . . . Drop it. Let's change subjects . . . What is this I hear about you and Ms. Brockhurst?" "I'm the luckiest guy in the world. She is lovely any way you look at her."

"That's good. Nothing beats love. I remember the day that you asked me who she was. Now, when you run that champion of yours, "A Sure Thing," in the Belmont. I'm going to pull myself together for that day, get out to see the race, and yell him home! Don't let me down . . . Good luck!" He reluctantly gave his wife a serious glance then looked back to his guest, "Ray, I don't want to chase you, but it is time for me to lie down. My strength is limited. Come back. It was thoughtful for you to visit again."

Upon leaving, the trainer took some comfort in the fact that his old friend still had a sharp mind and a good attitude. He could only respect and love Joe.

CHAPTER 23
Charles Objects

The large oak table in the combined mansion library and conference room was the gathering place for this family meeting requested by Suzanne. To Charles's right sat Isabel while across from them were Suzanne and Raymond, holding hands. Proudly, Suzanne confided to her parents, "Mom, Dad, we are here for a very special reason. I have something exciting to tell you . . . Raymond and I have been engaged for several days."

Charles's jaw dropped. Isabel's eyes lighted up in delight, then Charles regained his composure. "Congratulations—congratulations are not in order! I do not approve. This is all too fast." The caring other asked, "Suzanne dear, are you sure? Do you love each other?" "Yes, Mother. Never more certain about anything in my life." Raymond chimed in, "Suzanne said that for both of us. We would be happy together if stranded on an island" An adamant Charles protested, "Let me put a stop to this romantic nonsense my way! I've given it a lot of thought when you bought that colt for this fellow to train. Money was withdrawn from the inheritance left to you by your grandmother."

Defending herself, she said, "It wasn't the first time I touched the inheritance, and there never was an objection. You allowed withdrawals on other occasions." Giving Suzanne a bold side stare, he said, "Before I proceed any further, does this man have any idea of the wealth in your grandmother's estate?"

"No. He never asked. He doesn't care." "Good . . . Let's keep it that way. He has no right to know and—" Suzanne could not contain herself. "Dad, why are you doing this, talking about money at this time? No one was hurt, and A "Sure Thing" is a valuable Thoroughbred. I asked Raymond to join me at the sale. It was my idea, not his, and besides, look at the fine prospect we selected. Why are you so bitter?"

"Please don't interrupt. Let me continue. You needed my permission to withdraw any funds prior to your twenty-second birthday. "But Dad, it's my inheritance. Sooner or later, what is the difference?" "I will tell you difference; it is called . . . approval! Well, this did not happen in this case. For the colt's purchase, there wasn't any permission given from me for that large sum of money to be transferred. You weren't authorized . . . plain and simple!" "Wait a minute, Dad. Are you saying that I do not own the colt?"

"No, but all property you acquire through funds from the estate fall under my power of attorney until you reach twenty-two, unless otherwise agreed in advance. Well, that is not the case." "I am confused. What do you want?" "If this animal is to stay under this . . . this gigolo's care," Charles made sure that he was sitting perfectly straight as he gave the ultimatum, "Your engagement must be terminated immediately. You will see each other rarely and only on a strictly business basis. I stand firmly on that demand! It is not debatable!" Listening attentively, Raymond had been rocking slowly back and forth in his armchair, waiting for the Brockhurst hammer to hit him in the head. It was inevitable.

"May I speak?"

"Don't make it too long!" growled Charles.

"My feelings have always been above board, and the concept of being called a gigolo is unfounded. However, I love Suzanne, and that is all that counts!" "That was fast . . . You have sealed your own destiny. Tomorrow morning, the colt will leave your barn, transferred to Mr. Weatherbe." "Dad, how can you dare do this to me? Mother, say something, please."

Listening in profound embarrassment, Isabel finally spoke her piece, "Charles, you are sailing in uncharted waters. You should be ashamed. True love cannot be destroyed by a threat!" Charles stood his ground. "We will test how true is their love . . . One day, you all will thank me"— giving Raymond a prolonged antagonistic glare, "Even you!" Sadly, starting to cry, Suzanne looked at Raymond. He reached over, putting his arm around her while using the side of his thumb to gently wipe away the expressive tears.

Her father had crushed Suzanne at a moment of great joy, an engagement announcement. Whispering into Raymond's ear, she said, "This is so difficult. I must leave. My heart is breaking! Why this torture?" With tears falling over her cheeks, she glanced up to her parents. "Forgive me. I ask permission to leave." She quickly exited the library in a manner befitting a lady. There wasn't an outburst of temperament or idle threats.

With class and respect, Raymond asked if he might also be excused, but Charles was not finished with him. "I read the report relating to the shooting at your barn and the drugging incidents. The racing commission will hold a hearing on the matter. You better have all the right answers or else! Now, you are excused!" In Raymond's mind, the only place that he was excused to go was a jagged cliff from which he could jump.

The next day, Raymond arrived at the track and saw Suzanne sitting in the family box. They had not spoken since the previous evening, each one gathering their thoughts and trying to heal this terrible problem before they saw one another. He walked over. She was not aware of his presence until he reached her. "May I join you?" Surprised, she said, "Yes, dear. It should be alright."

"What does that mean?" "My father does not want me to see you ever. He forbids any relationship, and I don't know what we should do?" "I gave up the horse." Said Raymond, "His demand was satisfied." "As far as Dad is concerned, you made the wrong choice. He wanted you to give me up and keep the horse." Pausing, she carefully chose her words, "Father has the mentality of a sixteenth-century nobleman who wants his daughter to marry a future king." "I would like to oblige, but I'm a horse trainer, not a prince, yet I have a great love for the lovely lady locked in the castle tower."

"How sweet. That makes you, my knight. Still, discretion must be used when and where we meet. It must be secret." "Fine, but it shouldn't have to be that way. I gave up "A Sure Thing." A deal is a deal. It should be honored!" "Frustrating for me also. It would be best if you didn't stay any longer. Let us keep thinking of a way to solve a dilemma which keeps us apart." "Sure, darling. I'll go, so we don't alienate your father anymore."

Someday, with the help of a miracle . . . I will be his friend. He shall understand." "Our goal . . . I love you!" She blew him a silent kiss! "I'll be back after the hearing." "What hearing?" "With the racing commission. Today is my day in court." Suzanne was unaware of this event. "I did not know . . . Do well!"

Raymond was scheduled to appear at a three that same afternoon with the racing commission regarding the shooting incident at his barn, the attempted arson, and the drugging of Tenor. The tribunal included the racing commissioner, Mr. Wrigley Jones, the commission attorney, Mr. Josh Appleman; and the state steward, Mr. R. Lawrence Midland, representing the commission at the track. The party summoned to the hearing was allowed to be represented by an attorney and witnesses if any.

Raymond declined all privileges. His best witness would have been the respectable Dr. Matthews, his friend, and the last thing that either wanted to do was get him involved Of course, there was another witness living in Brooklyn. This man knew the whole story better than anyone, but how long would the racing officials remain in the room if Raymond brought Vito to the hearing? Oddsmakers in Las Vegas would have made the bet even money, favoring Vito alone in the room in less than five minutes!

The two main points that would be judged were, first, why was there violence at the track and potential damage to property that could have been avoided by notifying track security. Secondly, a drugged horse ran under his care and won a race. Both were serious charges, and the penalties ranged from a permanent denial of holding a trainer's license in New York or, in fact, anywhere; a suspension for X number of days, a monetary fine; or any combination of the last two mentioned options. The commission attorney, in a legal tone, started with the charge of participating in violence. He read the track security and police reports regarding the incident. Raymond concurred that the reports were correct, and he had nothing to add.

The judges moved on to the drugging issue. According to the trainer's Absolute Insurer Rule if a Thoroughbred showed a positive drug result after winning a race, the trainer was responsible. No excuses! However, in this case, nothing was found. "Tenor" had been treated with a designer drug, known as a performance-enhancing drug, which was not detected.

Only by Raymond's earlier statements did they became aware of an unknown substance being administered to "Tenor" by Bruno and Sonny. That scandal still had not been revealed to the press, and probably never would see daylight. The commission members asked Raymond to leave the room, so they might deliberate.

A half hour later, he was called back. The verdict was "A thousand dollar fine for the violent incident at the barn." Their judgment concluded, "Track security should've been notified and intervened! It is their professional purpose. Your license is to train horses, not shoot people!" The second allegation of drugging was far more complicated. The commission did not want to take any chance of an adverse decision being handed down from a civil court, possibly resulting in a sizeable lawsuit against the racetrack.

It was agreed that Raymond had little choice regarding the running of "Tenor." It was important for a racetrack to manage its integrity and image regarding drugging incidents, but there wasn't any long-term solution. The crooks with their tricky schemes were usually one step ahead of authority! Raymond's hearing was not the first of its kind. Drugging was embedded into the sport, but under the unique element of his case, no further investigation was required. The fact that Raymond had scratched two horses that were drugged weighed heavily in his favor. Other factors involving Alfredo's killers and jockeys fixing races were not a part of Raymond's trial, but the police department with the racetrack security would fully pursue those issues. They had to be resolved.

The trainer was relieved. He looked up to the ceiling! The judgment was concluded! It could have been career-ending! He was anxious to return to the box area and bring the good news back to his love, that he only received a fine and was exonerated from other issues before she heard the results from her father. He wanted her to be prepared for any different version that Mr. Brockhurst might present. At this point in their relationship, Raymond had no reason to place any trust in that man!

CHAPTER 24
Another Afternoon of Racing

Several days after Raymond gave Suzanne the commission results, she sat with Ashley in the clubhouse box where they were greeted by well- wishers. On the chair next to her was a daily racing newspaper. The headline read, "A Sure Thing" Wins the Mountain View Stakes easily for trainer Walter Weatherbe." A complimentary picture of the owner was set to the right side of the article.

One of the other people present was a female sports reporter, Sally Duhurst. She had written down numerous notes on a pad during her interview with Suzanne. Off in the distance, Raymond was observing the electric atmosphere surrounding Suzanne. As the reporter left that section, she noticed Raymond was alone and walked toward him, perhaps to find out if the story had a different twist.

"Hello, Raymond. May I talk with you?" "Sure, Sally. There's no waiting line. Please sit down." "Listen, I have two tough questions. How does it feel to have lost the derby's favorite? Maybe that opportunity comes along once in a lifetime if ever. Second question, how is your relationship with Mr. Brockhurst?" "The answers to your inquiry are not a problem . . . It's Suzanne's colt, and I wish her the best! She deserves it." "Are you sure it doesn't bother you?"

"Bother me doesn't exist. Suzanne is first in my life. I can't wish her anything but success and will always see that colt as my favorite! He has class and should continue to develop . . . About my relationship with Suzanne's dad . . . you would have to ask him." The reporter winked. "I listened to what you said and to what you didn't say, avoiding confrontation . . . Most people aren't that cautious. This has been an

145

interesting interview. You should be a reporter." They both smiled, withholding laughter. The reporter wrote nothing and put her pad away. She left Raymond to be again alone, returning to his innermost thoughts, which he was not sharing.

Three weeks later, the headlines on the racing newspaper read, "A Sure Thing" wins last two-year-old stake race of the season by 8 Lengths. A Solid Derby Favorite." Walking into the box section that day, Suzanne began searching carefully for Raymond. When the society celebrity spotted her mate, she walked over and, upon reaching him, touched his shoulder with warm, caring pressure.

He placed his hand on hers, saying, "You look so beautiful . . . Is it safe for us to be together?" "Yes. I have thought it out carefully, and there is only one dynamite answer to solve our problem. Can we have dinner at your apartment tonight?" "How about seven thirty?" he suggested. "Perfect. But please don't fuss."

"I'll order Chinese." "Sweetheart, you are so predictable." Both grinned. She parted from him with a "See you later, Chef." Evening arrived; the front doorbell rang, and Raymond responded quickly. With no surprise, it was the expected guest who gave him a robust hug and kiss. He acknowledged her warmth. "This night is starting off great." Sharing a thought, she said, "Everything is alright now. We are about to get past a toll taker. The bridge is open." "Bridge, toll taker? Woman, what are you talking about?" "Oh, only Ashley would understand that remark. I take it back. Too long to explain."

The host took Suzanne by the hand, bringing her to the living room couch. "Let's get comfortable, and you can tell me the answer to our puzzle." Raymond lay on the couch and placed his head on her lap. She delicately stroked her fingers through his hair. He became romantically inclined. "We have so much love to share." However, the lady's thoughts went in a different direction. She wanted to discuss her reason for getting together. Romance was placed on the sidelines, at least for a little while. She had him sit up straight. "How would you like to be "A Sure Thing's" trainer for the Derby?" The lover was caught off guard. "Don't tease me. Please don't." Raymond tickled her side; she wiggled and giggled. "No teasing.

Stop making me laugh . . . What day is the Derby and what is May 5?" "The day before May 6." This smart remark earned him a wake-up nudge on the head. "You do not know, do you? On May 5, I am twenty-two, and the Derby is scheduled for May 6. On that day . . . I own the horse with no impediments. My father is legally out of the picture!" An amazed Raymond said, "I like what I'm hearing. Fate! What a powerful, overwhelming force is fate!" "I have covered all the bases, spoken to my lawyer, and Dad's power of attorney is terminated a day before the Derby . . . and I can return "A Sure Thing" to you on Derby Day! This will show Dad how serious I am about our relationship, and you will get back what you never should have lost."

"You, me, and "A Sure Thing" . . . together again! I can't believe it. We must start preparing now for the road ahead. Maybe a Triple Crown run. There are going to be some hectic weeks in the future." Getting comfortable, he placed his arm over Suzanne's shoulder. As she rubbed the back of his neck, the lady reached over, turning the lamp light off. There was no rush for dinner and no more need for horse talk about the future. Romance was in the offering even though the Chinese food was getting cold.

CHAPTER 25
The Triple Crown Campaign

The makeup of the Triple Crown consists of three races. The first springtime challenge, on the first Saturday of May, is the one-mile-and-one-quarter Kentucky Derby in Louisville, Kentucky. The one-mile-and-three-sixteenth Preakness is held at Pimlico Racecourse in Baltimore, Maryland, two weeks later. The final jewel in the crown, three weeks after the Preakness, is the mile and one- half Belmont run at Belmont Park, Elmont, New York. Three races in three different states over a five-week period are an exceptional challenge for any horse, even more so for a relatively young three-year-old Thoroughbred.

What are some of the drawbacks? Most of the Thoroughbreds ship to Churchill Downs, so they may participate in the Run for the Roses; some coming from as far west as California or perhaps even from a foreign country. Placing a racehorse on a plane or van for a long ride from anywhere has risk factors. A trip can be delayed at an airport for hours or a van might break down or be in an accident. During their time of traveling, they are confined to tight quarters and not nearly as comfortable or relaxed as they would be in a stall. They might catch a cold from a draft, and for certain, normal feeding schedules and training routines are nonexistent.

Bottom line, some Thoroughbreds ship better than others, and some are subject to fewer travel complications than their competitors. All in all, there is also a home field advantage for any horses that are already stabled at one of the racetracks hosting a Triple Crown event. They have no traveling issues and are familiar with the racing surface and layout of the grounds. Back to those who must ship. The air quality in a van or airplane is quite different from what they are used to breathing in a barn environment or outdoors. Human passengers can become sick from travel, and so can racehorses. Ultimately, they are flesh and blood like us with one huge difference. They weigh a thousand pounds or more.

After their initial trip to Kentucky, they must move five hundred miles or so from Kentucky to Maryland and, eventually, complete the odyssey adventure from there to the Big Apple. The weather also plays a role. The first May Saturday in Kentucky may be a pleasant spring day or cold and rainy, resulting in a muddy racing strip. Some horses thrive better in certain weather conditions than others. Luck plays a big part in the outcome of these uncontrollable factors. As it is said, "You are at the mercy of the weather."

The above mentioned are some reasons along with high caliber competition, that decades may pass before the challenge to win a Triple Crown is realized. In 1919, Sir Barton was the first horse to win all three races and was retroactively given the title of Triple Crown winner. The concept of "Triple Crown" was formally proclaimed in December 1950 in New York City at the Awards Dinner of the Thoroughbred Racing Association. Only thirteen horses have realized the taste of that elusive victory.

The trail described above was part of a two-year racing journey for the twenty Thoroughbred racehorses running in the Triple Crown races. The start for all these horses began in the breeding shed where artificial insemination is not permitted. The breeder may be commercial or an individual intending to race or sell. The number of foals each year rises or drops, depending on the financial stability and predictions of the industry's health. The swing can range from amazing optimism to an extremely cautious projection with a downward rate in foal numbers. In the past twenty-five years, the yearly production rate has swayed from the high thirty thousand foals to the low twenties.

The option for most breeders is to place their stock as yearlings, or two-year-old, in a sale. If the reserve that they set is not met, the stock is taken back home. On that note, they can enter other venues or sell to an individual privately or, as a last choice, race it themselves. This is not what the commercial breeder wants. The present cost of keeping a Thoroughbred in training for one year in New York is over forty thousand dollars. Going to a commercial auction, Raymond and Suzann bid on and purchased "A Sure Thing" to race. At that point, both breeder and buyer got what they wanted, a perfect marriage. The breeder was satisfactorily compensated for his investment, and luckily, they got a high-caliber

individual. The moment of truth had arrived for the crop in which "A Sure Thing" was foaled. It was Kentucky Derby time. Only one could win. Each horse had been well prepared; each would give its all!

CHAPTER 26
The Derby

It was Derby Day, May 6, one month after their eventful Chinese dinner. Raymond and Suzanne were standing in the Kentucky Derby stakes barn, waiting for the loudspeaker to call, "Bring your horses to the paddock." The tension mounted by the second, even for the finely dressed lady, whose colorful wide-brim hat, decorated with pheasant feathers, could easily be the winner of the Best Hat Contest held on Derby Day. That was not the prize she came to win.

At the track, Charles and Isabel sat and chatted with others in a special box area assigned to racetrack owners. The total wealth spread out among this group was incalculable. A bold announcement came over the loudspeaker. Announcer: "There will be a program change in the Kentucky Derby. Number 14, "A Sure Thing's" trainer will be Raymond Masterson." The crowd roared approval by cheering. They knew the bizarre story behind the horse's history, siding with Raymond and the lovely Ms. Brockhurst.

Charles dropped his head. "I knew this was coming. Our lawyer had informed me." Isabel, slightly surprised, queried, "Why didn't you tell me?" "Because I was ashamed! Didn't know how to. Didn't want too either. It would have happened regardless and that was that. I apologize." Isabel was graceful. "I understand." The Derby horses soon were called to the paddock, each one accompanied by its groom, hot-walker, owner or representative, and trainer. Selected press members were in the mix. Raymond with the favorite in the derby was the center of attention for reporters.

"How does it feel to have your horse back?" Not wanting to be controversial at this moment, he felt that an evasive answer was best, "It is a tremendous thrill to be here." In short order, another media person shouted a similar question, "Are you happy that the horse is under your care?" "A Sure Thing" was always in my heart. He never left!" Suzanne loved that response, and her face warmly glowed.

As the horses were being saddled, the density of the crowd around the paddock was immeasurable. Twenty of the finest three-year-old's were there to compete in the most prestigious race in the world, the Kentucky Derby. All the patrons had their favorite Thoroughbred, trainer or special jockey. The buzz of opinions hummed through the crowd. Freedom to speak their minds prevailed, and it didn't matter if they were betting two dollars or two thousand dollars.

Everyone's opinion in the crowd was valid. The Irish have an interesting saying about equality, "All men are created equal above and below the ground." The racehorses had been ceremonially saddled, and the call, "Riders up," was sung out by a country-and-western star. The twenty magnificent Thoroughbreds pranced onto the track to the tune of "My Old Kentucky Home."

The warmup period was ample, and at post time, the entire field of anxious three-year-old's was placed in two starting gates. Each Thoroughbred had an assistant starter assigned to it and the break was initiated immediately after the last horse was loaded. Announcer: "They are off! The running of the Ninety-Third Kentucky Derby has begun! A clean break for all except "Real Offense" and "Wister," who bump at the start and have dropped back." "What a cavalry charge. This is a race that needs a prayer for everyone's safety, riders, and horses," was Suzanne's observation.

Although she had been there before, her nerves were on edge She now owned the favorite! The game plan for Jockey Kelly worked well in the early stages, drop over to the rail from his number 14 post position, be placed somewhere in the middle of the pack, and save ground, while reserving his mount for a bold stretch run. He was not going to let his mount got caught up in an early speed duel and fade in the stretch.

As the field turned for home, a quarter of a mile to the finish line, the perfect ride went haywire! Announcer: "The favorite, "A Sure Thing" is buried on the rail." Agreeing with the announcer, Raymond yelled, "We are shut off. The colt needs some room somewhere!" "He appears to be full of run," observed Suzanne. Jockey Kelly said a little prayer, "God, part the traffic. Show me away home!" The jockey, in his moment of desperation, could not help but thoughtfully add, "I'll never ask for anything again." Announcer: "The favorite is trying to squeeze through on the rail." Kelly's boot was scrapping white paint off the inner rail as he held his position and waited to make a run at the leaders.

Announcer: "A Sure Thing" is looking for a hole which isn't there!" At that precise moment, Jockey Kelly shouted to the rider in front of him, luckily an old friend, Bobby Torrin, "Bobby . . . I need room, or I'm going down. Help me!" That jockey in front quickly looked inside, saw the critical situation, and acknowledged, "Steve, my horse is tiring. I'll give what I can, but it ain't gonna be much!"

Jockey Bobby moved his mount over barely enough for the Favorite to bully his way through the seam. Announcer: "Rare Event" — "War Eagle" head- to- head on the outside . . . Yes! "A Sure Thing" fought his way through, flying on the rail." The gallant thoroughbred dropped his head and soon had the freedom to use his long, powerful legs, picking them up and setting them down. The ground that he was traveling on disappeared in a flash! Announcer: "The finish line. "A Sure Thing" all out by a neck. Photo for second. Hold all pari-mutuel tickets until the result is official." The board lighted up quickly. "Suzanne owned the winner, "War Eagle," second . . . "Rare Event" third."

A numb I-can't-believe-it feeling came over Raymond and Suzanne. In another box, Charles and Isabel showed uncontrolled exhilaration. "Charles, is this not wonderful? What are you going to do now?" "Surrender!" Isabel viewed the young couple moving in their direction. "Here comes Suzanne and Raymond." Standing erect, Charles pulled back his shoulders. The man didn't know what to expect. This could be an in-your-face moment. Receiving congratulations from all sides, the victorious couple advanced to her parents. Everyone wanted to shake their hands or touch the winners.

Giving her mother a kiss, Suzanne said, "Mom, Dad, please join us in the winner's circle." Isabel was gracious. "So lovely you asked us." This painless invitation was a great relief for Charles. All four were guided by security officers through a multitude of cheering people on the way to the festive infield ceremony. Arriving at that area, a sincere handshake was given by Charles to Raymond, then another and another. "I have been completely wrong about you, son. Raymond, you are all right in my book. Can you accept my apology?" "You did what you believed to be right. I always respected that." The young trainer sought no retribution and his kind attitude found favor with Charles. The new friends shook hands again, with joyful expression.

Happily watching while the healing of the men took place, Isabel and Suzanne were thrilled. Softly, she told her daughter, "Peace at last!" Standing side by side with them in the Churchill Downs Winner's Circle, Charles was finally reunited with his family. Cameras flashed and reporters waited for the sports story of the year. That group was all smiles as they watched their Champion, the crowd's favorite, prance around the winner's circle. An attractive blanket of red roses was placed over the colt's dancing shoulders.

Holding his head straight up, Jockey Kelly continually raised his arms skyward in a pumping motion to display a true thanksgiving to God! For Kelly, this victory was unquestionably a miracle! The records would now show that his name was listed next to the great winning riders of the past. Be it known he had only ridden in one previous Derby.

Raymond and Suzanne shouted above the crowd's noise for their Jockey to hear them, "Great ride. It was spectacular!" He waved his whip in their direction, and captivated by the victory, he cried out to them, "Triple Crown, Triple Crown!" Everyone in the winner's circle paid attention and joined in the chant. The crowd began to form an echo, "Triple Crown! Triple Crown!" Also caught up in the magic of the moment, a joyful Charles waved to the crowd as if he was running for a political position, shouting back to them, "Let's go for it! Why not? Yes! Yes! Yes!"

CHAPTER 27
The Morning After

*I*t was eight o'clock the morning after the Derby as Raymond and Suzanne drove to the barn. Andre greeted them, "Buenos dias." In an encouraging way, he said, "He ate everything. Is happy." This information pleased the owner. "That's a great start, but can he hold his form and weight for two more difficult races?" "That's my job to make it happen," then Raymond added wistfully, "With a little bit of luck."

All trainers know that it takes only one misstep, or only one mistake to destroy the dream. It could come from him or from the jockey or a stone on the ground or any number of possibilities. It is well known, regarding any race, there is just one way to win and one hundred ways to lose it! Their horse peered out of the stall toward them, snorted once while his beautiful eyes surveyed the surroundings with self-importance. He was the king!

The trainer had his lovely lady, who was showing her shapely legs, get comfortable in one of the two folding beach chairs, which he had placed on the grass area outside of the barn, in front of "A Sure Thing's" stall. Raymond excused himself, walking to the track kitchen, which wasn't far away, and purchased two coffees and, mind you, two donuts! They were not counting calories. Their waistlines were perfect! Was there a more serene place in the world to be? With the celebrity moment behind them, this was the time to unwind, relax, be alone, and hold hands under a peek from the rising sun. Life does not get any better.

After their stay at the racetrack, the couple enjoyed a drive around town, stopping at the Triumph House Museum. This historic Victorian mansion was in the heart of Old Louisville on Avery St. Admiring the wonderful construction, they were captivated by the amazing works of art. The Tiffany windows produced glows of warmth, and sculpted mahogany wood comfortably embraced the stairways and high ceilings.

The breathtaking Carrara marble fireplaces throughout the striking 1888 Romanesque building accented that period's architecture. Their visit to this style of Victorian house brought back fond memories of the summer that she spent with the Good Sisters of Mercy in Louisiana. The structures were as different as night and day, but Victorian is Victorian. Returning for lunch at the Liberty Hotel, where they were staying, Suzanne pondered, "Our lives are so full of excitement! We are so fortunate . . . What more could we ask, dear?"

"The best of all, is out there . . . waiting for us. It is the greatest of treasures." What was Raymond thinking about? Hardly able to wait for the brilliant explanation, she asked, "How, my dear?" "Sweetheart . . . let's get married! Sharing love, caring for one another for the rest of our lives. What could be more meaningful?"

That marvelous, romantic answer was not expected. "What! Darling, . . . you must know my parents have always planned for their only child to have a fashionable wedding at Saint Patrick's and the reception at the Waldorf. Nothing else would be suitable for them, and I don't have a problem with their wishes. This type of wedding is every girl's dream!"

"Baby, do it my way for now. After the Belmont, we can plan it properly—a church ceremony, a big affair, whatever makes you happy . . . It's a promise . . . Your joy will be my joy!" "Raymond, who is crazy now? "Me! Crazy in love with you, and the pressure of the Triple Crown makes desire unbearable. Having you as my wife, being together forever . . . is more important than anything else!"

"Our lives are moving fast, but you just broke the sound barrier. Let me sleep on it." That evening as they lay in bed in each other arms, Suzanne whispered into his ear. Raymond returned it with a whisper of his own, "This is all a dream. How can it be real?" "Want to be sure? Go ahead. Pinch me and find out." He did, she yelled, and both jumped! Gathering themselves they returned with loving words to a motionless embrace. Deciding to keep "A Sure Thing" in Kentucky for five days after the derby, Raymond was giving their colt ample time to fully regain his strength. The derby win was not an easy victory and the stretch drive was all out strenuous.

A trainer with keen observations and solid decision-making regarding the condition of Thoroughbreds in his charge will have them performing at peak form, and they will win their share of races. Even a quality horse takes time to recover, and each situation can and will be different from the previous one. Therefore, correct choices had to be made, and that was the responsibility of a trainer. Sometimes they had to refute suggestions from a well-intentioned owner who had ideas on how to train or in what race to run their horse. On more than one occasion, this conflict caused a trainer to lose the account. Luckily, Suzanne did not fall into this category.

It was clearly stated that wherever her colt was, she would also be there. In no uncertain terms, she expressed her position, "If he stays here five days, and you stay, I stay!" Raymond gave her an up-and-down glance. "I should make you my assistant trainer." Acting sexy, which required no effort, she threw out her right hip and slowly rubbed her hand over it, "Can you afford me?" "Nope." This was a close-knit team; they dreamed together and being together produced the magic.

After the five days of rest, relaxation, and two easy gallops, "A Sure Thing" was ready to be loaded on a private van headed to Maryland. There were just nine days to the Preakness, and Raymond wanted his horse to become familiar with the Pimlico surroundings, training over that track's surface with at least one timed workout. At the last minute, Raymond informed Suzanne that he would ride in the van with the colt from Kentucky to Maryland. "I want to ride with you. Don't go alone. You said that you were crazy about me, and now I'm being abandoned." She forced herself not to laugh.

"It isn't ladylike to ride in a horse van," reminded her lover. The female knew that her boyfriend was correct. There wasn't a lady's restroom on a horse van, only straw on the floor. Extremely unladylike.

"Don't worry. When I get to Maryland, I will show you how lonely I am." "You better!" she asserted. Raymond and "A Sure Thing" arrived in Maryland, after an uneventful trip accompanied by a police escort, Suzanne was waiting for him at the unloading ramp. Their young faces beamed happiness, they really didn't want to be apart.

Andre took his charge into a special designated stakes barn, to stall number 1, which was reserved for the Kentucky Derby victor. Soon alone, it was time for her to be romantic, "Remember your Let's get married' idea." "The only thing I had on my mind for the past five hundred plus miles while on the bouncing van. Are you ready to give an answer?" "The answer is yes!" They embraced! With Suzanne at his side, Raymond worked out his barn schedule so that they would have an afternoon available to take the vows and have the next twenty-four hours free for each other.

Four days later, after obtaining a license to be joined, they were married in an unpretentious ceremony, but beautiful for them, at a courthouse in Baltimore, Maryland. No photographers, no fanfare, no thrown rice, but plain and simple true love, be it ever so humble. However, the wedding kiss was a record breaker. Their marriage included a War World II–type military honeymoon—a one-day whirlwind! Since they were in Maryland where else to enjoy their newfound unity but at the Baltimore Inner Harbor, located on the point where the Patapsco River estuary flows into the Chesapeake Bay.

Nearby, eight minutes away, stood the national monument and historic shrine, Fort McHenry, the inspirational location for Francis Scott Key's poem, "The Star-Spangled Banner," written in September 1814. A Congressional Resolution in 1931, signed by President Herbert Hoover, made it the national anthem.

The first act was to book a hotel room, and although pleasant, it was not a honeymoon suite; however, for these lovers, a tent would have sufficed. They did a little shopping where Suzanne bought a stylish spring hat and Raymond two ties. Enough of stores, time was short for the couple to enjoy their first day of marriage. Washington DC was only forty miles away, but they were not seeking to subtract driving time from an already limited schedule. They wanted to hold hands or be in each other's caresses.

Their wedding dinner consisted of Maryland crab cakes, fries, and a salad along with champagne. Sitting at an outside table they enjoyed the evening bay breeze drifting in from the harbor. This charming restaurant, bordering on the edge of the lighted water place, was at full capacity that night, so the lovers decided to consider all those patrons as special wedding guests. Making an imaginary party, saying hello to many was fun, and who cared if there weren't any gifts? To their surprise, their early twenties waitress had a strong Southern accent and when asked about it she gave them the reason. Her answer could not have been guessed.

The newlyweds were told that although Maryland did not secede from the Union, a Southern part of Maryland sided with the Confederacy during the Civil War. To this day that pocket of the population still spoke with a distinctive Southern drawl. History lessons are endless. Chronologically speaking and tracing back to the 1700s, this harbor was an active warehouse port area, which slowly transitioned through the decades to an entertainment district for tourists, who came in increasing numbers to enjoy it. They returned the next day to again visit that renowned location.

The main attraction in this scenic harbor was the USS Constellation, a sloop, commissioned in 1854, and now a historical monument. A tall, white sail, warship built for the North, she is recognized as being the largest ship of its kind commissioned by the Union, and the only one of its kind to still be afloat Slipping back over a hundred years they strolled on its wooden decks. Suzanne was deeply impressed with the ship's antiquity, the whispering white sails, and the shined bronze canons.

Out of the blue, she rendered a random thought to her husband, "Captain, could you imagine sailing one of these?" Only one reservation came from the captain, "Sure, sweetheart. What flag will you fly?" With hands joined, they continually hugged affectionately and sneaked in a kiss here and there from an unlimited supply. While enjoying and walking through this historical area, their hearts both truly longed for their hotel room, which was the centerpiece of any short, romantic honeymoon. Returning midnoon to the hotel, they enjoyed one more hour in their love cave before packing up and heading back to the racetrack.

A strong possibility loomed that, in nine months, their family would be increased by one. These moments were magical for the duo. A reception and a lengthy honeymoon would properly follow. However, that affair was the last thought on either mind; they were husband and wife, and a Triple Crown challenge was on the horizon. It would be impossible to fit anything of equal importance into that itinerary. Their portrait could find no room for additional colors.

CHAPTER 28
The Preakness

*I*t was the running of the Ninety-Second Preakness. Well over one hundred thousand partying patrons, many with beer in hand and in the infield area, were on hand to see a possible Triple Crown champion pursue his legacy. The outside saddling area on the grass course at Pimlico not only gave more room for the participants to be saddled, but of equal importance, the racehorses were in full view of all the spectators. This presented a different scene from the other two Triple Crown racetracks where the Thoroughbreds were saddled inside stalls and walked around a circular paddock located in the back of the stands.

The horses seemed to be more at ease in this spacious, natural setting. Unfortunately, the Brockhursts were not able to be with their daughter for the Preakness. Charles was the guest speaker at a business convention held in Phoenix, Arizona, that very same day; therefore, Suzanne and her husband stood alone, waiting for Steve Kelly.

Suzanne asked, 'What do you have on your mind to tell our jockey?' "Nothing. You know I don't tell a rider how to ride. Any advice will only complicate matters." "That is why Steve likes to ride for you because you don't weigh him down with instructions."

When they arrived all the jockeys greeted the involved parties, walked over to their mounts and were given a leg up. Steve's mount was post position seven in a field of eleven. Seven of the contenders ran against him on the Derby, and the other three were newcomers all trying to pull off an upset. "War Eagle," the close runner up in the derby, was seeking a reversal of fortunes. When the field paraded to the track, the band played, "Maryland, My Maryland." Those in attendance stood in quiet respect.

All vested parties, by this time, had returned to the box area, where they anticipated the call of the race. The wait was over. Announcer: "It's post time." Again, all the spectators rose to their feet, and in short order, the horses came flying out of the gate, but "A Sure Thing" stumbled, grabbing a quarter on his right front foot. This happens when the toe of a hind horseshoe hits the back quarter of a front hoof.

Blood appeared immediately over the area. Jockey Kelly sensed that the horse was not settling into his usual smooth stride but didn't know why. Being an experienced jockey and knowing his mount, he decided to take it easy and see how this Thoroughbred managed to overcome whatever was bothering him. Would it go away or get worse? There was no way to tell.

As they went into the first turn, the clubhouse turn, Kelly still waited for the horse to give him the answer. There was none. Down the backstretch, nothing changed. The jockey still had to be patient. At last, near the half-mile pole, "A Sure Thing" pricked his ears forward and began to try to be competitive, but sheer will, guts, and breeding could not overcome the sharp pain that he felt in his foot. Suzanne, Raymond, and the crowd were uncertain why the three -year- old was running that type of race. They were concerned but helpless.

Talking to his mount, Kelly said, "Boy, what is wrong? Seconds passed, and finally, the jockey felt that although "A Sure Thing" was trying hard, he couldn't get into a comfortable stride. Kelly was not able to comprehend the amount of fresh blood escaping out from the wound, blood that shortly before had pumped through his mount's gallant heart. The favorite finished in the middle of the pack, beaten seven lengths. The California horse, "War Eagle," had easily won. As he was being unsaddled, the Thoroughbred pawed the ground, blood spattering on to it.

A disheartened Raymond with Suzanne at his side began to care for their horse as soon as the injured animal got back to the barn. Upon examination, the trainer and Andre did what was immediately necessary. Hair was cut away from the gash, then washed out with soap and warm water, followed by peroxide, and tapped dry with sterilized absorbent cotton. Suzanne bit her lips several times while watching the procedure,

Finally, Andre placed a thick square, gauzed-covered cotton patch saturated with Furacin, an antibiotic salve, over the wound and then wrapped an Ace bandage around it. The injury had been thoroughly cleaned, dressed, and protected. That evening, Raymond called Dr. Matthews and his New York blacksmith at their homes. They agreed to drive down to Maryland together and arrive there the next morning to confer. Raymond was anxious to be on top of the situation and knew the team that he was counting on would not let him down.

Not taking any chances on wasting time and taking advantage of the veterinarian's and blacksmith's valuable expertise was the foremost thought in the trainer's mind. This Thoroughbred had to dance one more dance, the Belmont, and it had to be perfect! The New Yorkers arrived in Maryland at eight A.M. and after the three-and-a-half-hour drive, they found Raymond and Suzanne waiting anxiously. The vet and the blacksmith, side by side, examined the horse. The first observations, properly, came from Dr. Matthews, "I believe the wound is manageable. You got lucky here. It could have been a lot worse, but get him a tetanus and anti-biotic shots just in case Continue the treatment that you started."

The same answer came from the blacksmith. "I'll keep checking as needed when you get back to Belmont, but I agree with Doc. You're gonna be alright. It's not too deep." Inquiring, the vet asked, "When are you coming to Belmont?" "Tomorrow. I want to be near both of you." "By week's end, the colt should be able to go back to the track," said the blacksmith.

It was what the trainer wanted to hear. "That won't hurt his training schedule. My horse is dead fit." After the vet and blacksmith left, the lady firmly related her most important concern to Raymond, "If he is not one hundred percent, I don't want him to run!" Raymond was of the same mindset. "It won't be any other way." Near the end of the week, Raymond felt confident to send his charge for easy exercise going the wrong way on the far outside of the track. He told the colt's regular exercise rider, Marko, that if anything didn't feel right, to pull him up and immediately bring him home.

The nonchalant jog went smoothly, and each day, the training level increased to everyone's satisfaction. The Derby winner seemed to be ready; however, they did not lose sight that, in morning training, the stress or pounding of the real race cannot be duplicated. There was always a question mark, which had to be best answered by a trainer's experience, daily observations, consultations, and lots of hope. A key person involved in a Thoroughbred's evaluation is the exercise rider. He is on the colt's back and can expertly report on the horse's soundness to the trainer.

CHAPTER 29
The Belmont

The paddock was packed with owners, guests, trainers, the press, and jockeys who occupied every inch of it. Jockey Kelly had to make several shifty, behind-the-line moves to reach Raymond and Suzanne. When he got to their location, the rider mused, "I hope that there isn't as much traffic in the race." The racing association had extensively promoted this race as the best from the East, "A Sure Thing", against the best from the West, "War Eagle." The Belmont would decide a champion. The attendance was huge to see the Derby winner face the colt that had beaten him soundly in the Preakness. The field total was twelve, with four starters that had not run in either of the other two races.

Speaking confidently with his rider, Raymond said, "I can't tell you anything but have a safe winning ride. It's up to you." A pumped-up jockey let the words fly out, "I was born for today!'" The paddock judge called, "Riders up!" As the Thoroughbreds reached the track, the band started to play, "The Sidewalks of New York." The crowd rose, sang along. Raymond and Suzanne had gone to the chairman's box with her parents and Ashley, who had invited a new boyfriend to join them. They were seated a few minutes and settled in when a young man approached the box from the far-right direction, weaving his way past people before reaching the back of the Brockhurst's private box.

He quietly called, "Mr. Masterson, Mr. Masterson." No one in the box heard him. The crowd around them was loud and they themselves were preoccupied. The fifteen- year-old young man spoke again, this time louder, "Mr. Masterson!" That did the trick. He was heard. Raymond turned sideways. "Did someone call me?" "I did, sir. Do you have a minute?" "Always have a minute. What's up?" "I am Mason Hardy." "Hey, Mason, heard great stories about you from your grandfather. Did he bring you to the races? "No, sir. My grandfather died last night." Caught off guard, Raymond was speechless for several seconds. "He died? "Yes, sir, and I am here specially to give you something that he wanted you to have." Mason raised a brown paper bag that he had at his side, opened the top, taking out a faded black binocular case.

He slowly lifted a pair of binoculars from it and handed them to Raymond. Staring at them, Raymond had a flashback to the first time he ever saw them around Joe Hardy's neck. "My father brought me to the races today in order that I could bring them to you. Please, please take the binoculars. My grandfather wanted you to have them." "With pride. I will use them today and every day. Tell your grandmother and parents that we deeply share in their loss. Your grandfather was an exceptional man. You should grow up to be just like him!" Mason blushed. Suzanne also expressed, "Mason, be kind to give your family our sympathy."

Raymond closed his eyes in respect, capturing a short remembrance of his departed friend. He placed his own new binoculars into the rack at the front of the box and swung Joe's over his head. Mason smiled. His grandfather's wish had been fulfilled. The shy youngster said goodbye to the group, moving away as unpretentiously as he had arrived and was quickly lost in the crowd. Suzanne found it touching. "How moving. Joe would have been so proud of his grandson. What a fine, presentable young boy."

The trainer was still trying to come to terms with the sad news. "This isn't easy to handle. That man was special to me. Give me a second to get myself together." A thought suddenly came to him, "Suzanne dear, if we win the Belmont, let's dedicate the trophy to Joe." The lady more than understood. She applauded the concept. "That would certainly be a heartfelt gesture." They then turned their attention again to the track as the field was about to enter the gate. The moment of truth presented itself again! Announcer: "Their set, ready . . . And they are off!"

Steve knew what he wanted to do—execute the textbook race: break well, lay off the pace, pulling away at the end in that exact order. This was a mile-and-a-half race and had to be ridden in a certain way. Again, his mount was not standing properly and did not break well. The assistant starter in the colt's stall was pulling backward on the reign to straighten him up, just as the starter sprang the latch. This caused the animal's head to shoot upward, resulting in his body being off balance and causing an awkward start.

The rider's mind had to again react quickly—should he rush "A Sure Thing" up was for the position that he desired, or let the colt relax and play catch-up. Smartly deciding on the latter, the jockey relaxed his mount. Announcer: "As the horses fly into the backstretch, the New York favorite is trailing the field and is going to keep us in suspense." Kelly had quickly adjusted his game plan, to wait, picking them off one by one. He could feel that an energetic "A Sure Thing" was under him, and he had a mile and a half to get it right.

Announcer: "Coming to the half-mile pole, the co-favorite still last." The owner and trainer wished it was otherwise but wishing and reality didn't always coincide. "A Sure Thing" and his jockey were on the same page. It was go time. One by one, his mount easily, comfortably, moved past rivals; and at the top of the stretch, with a quarter of a mile remaining, there were only two horses, four lengths, in front of him, the powerful "War Eagle" being one of them.

Announcer: "Kelly finally got what he wanted, moving effortlessly into third place." His jockey kept him in the middle of the racetrack and flew past the front runners.

Announcer: "It is all over. Only an eighth of a mile to the finish line, and "A Sure Thing" is pulling away!" The roar of the crowd was increasing. Announcer: "Winning like a true champion! "A Sure Thing" wins the Belmont by ten lengths. "War Eagle" a distant second!" The crowd went wild. The New Yorkers had backed the Eastern contender, and he had won! They were financially and thrillingly rewarded for their loyalty.

The lovers embraced one another. Only the embrace mattered! Predictably, the screams of the crowd too quickly brought them back to reality. Suzanne leaned away from Raymond, confiding, "How fortunate am I to have "A Sure Thing" twice in my life and both at the same time." "How lucky for me to be one of them, and I am not the least bit jealous of the famous one." Giving him an Academy Award look and kiss, they departed for the winner's circle ceremony. Raymond held her hand in his right hand with Joe Hardy's binoculars firmly in the other.

The winner's circle area was filled with dignitaries. The New York governor, the city mayor, the racing hierarchy, prominent guests, and the press were in jubilant attendance, sharing the victory. The owner, trainer and jockey received the usual accolades with sincere poise. Everyone was talking, giving their version of the brilliant win, but those who bet on "War Eagle" were talking to themselves.

On the immediate outside perimeter of the ceremonial winner's circle, a multitude of excited fans cheered, jumping up and down. There, among them, stood a quiet man wearing a long-sleeved white shirt, smoking a "Maduro Robusto" cigar. Seemingly alone in a sea of people, he was oblivious to the crowd around him, however; that lone well-wisher sported a glowing, giant smile of satisfaction greater than anyone else.

Continuing to receive countless congratulations, Raymond and Suzanne graciously accepted. "Thank you . . . Thank you . . . Thank you," a phrase repeated by them more times than could ever have been counted. As the heavy Belmont Trophy was placed in Raymond's hands, he sought Suzanne's participation in sharing to raise it as high as possible. As the crowd waited for Raymond to speak, he hesitated, clearing his throat, for he was overwhelmed with emotions, even showing soft tears. "Words cannot express how my wife and I feel today . . . We thank you all for being here."

Partially covering his mouth, Charles excitedly whispered to Isabel, "Wife! What wife?" As usual, Isabel was unflappable. "Quiet, dear. Enjoy the ceremony. They will tell us all about the marriage when they are ready." Raymond continued, "We would like to dedicate this Belmont Trophy to the memory of an amazing person who passed away last night."

The noise level in the crowd had significantly begun to lower. They were surprisingly paying attention. "I speak of Mr. Joe Hardy, a friend, a fine gentleman, a successful, honest horseman. You all knew of him. Joe trained Thoroughbreds at this very racetrack for close to thirty years. He was a special man. The kind of person we would all like to be. He cared about others, always found generous time for each of us. And . . . if it had not been for Joe, I wouldn't be standing here today. He made my success possible . . . That is the truth!"

Pausing for a moment, Raymond lifted his blue eyes upward to the sky, and again with Suzanne, raised the trophy along with the departed trainer's binoculars. Bidding his final farewell, he said, "We pray that Joe Hardy rests in peace and sleeps with the angels." Gently taking the microphone from Raymond's hand, Suzanne closed the tribute, "May God bless you, Mr. Hardy." Among fifty-two thousand fans, bowed heads prevailed, and the only sound that could be heard was silence.

--The End--

www.ingramcontent.com/pod-product-compliance
Lightning Source LLC
Chambersburg PA
CBHW072135300726

48975CB00003B/1067